Rowland Hussey Allen

The New-England Tragedies in Prose

Rowland Hussey Allen

The New-England Tragedies in Prose

ISBN/EAN: 9783337076467

Printed in Europe, USA, Canada, Australia, Japan

Cover: Foto ©Andreas Hilbeck / pixelio.de

More available books at **www.hansebooks.com**

THE

NEW-ENGLAND TRAGEDIES

IN PROSE.

BY

ROWLAND H. ALLEN.

BOSTON:

NICHOLS AND NOYES.

1869.

GEO. C. RAND & AVERY,
STEREOTYPERS AND PRINTERS,
3 CORNHILL, BOSTON.

PREFACE.

THE verse of Longfellow has been inspired again by the Muse of History. His theme is not a sportive one. The hand which has been wont to charm us with its blithe and joyous play, in this new motion sets ten thousand hearts athrob to the cadences of complaint. Yet our beloved poet does not disown himself. Ever and anon this minor melody gives way to the bright-toned, familiar calls of charity and candor.

To such laments for the two faults of the Fathers, we will listen without repining ; for we can foster the silent hope, meanwhile, that the next strain we hear will be one of noble praise for their grand and myriad virtues.

Till then we shall be curious to know how much is fact, and how much fancy, in the latest work of the "Laureate of America."

Mount Bellingham, November, 1868.

3

I.

The Coming of the Quakers.

5

THE
NEW-ENGLAND TRAGEDIES
IN PROSE.

———•———

I.

THE COMING OF THE QUAKERS.

JOHN ENDICOTT had the heart of a prince. He "came over to governe." He led the sturdy band that conquered from the domain of the forests the first free State of New England. And he "was a fit instrument to begin this wildernesse work." From his little ship, "The Abigail," he leaped upon the rocks of Naumkeak, less than eight years after "The Mayflower" anchored in Plymouth Bay. Three or four Englishmen only had ventured before that into the region around Cape Ann. They had fishing and trading posts there, but could hardly be said to have homes. They were, however, jealous of their rights ; and contention quickly kindled against the strangers. But

the new leader was **"loving as well as** austere ;"
and he dealt so gently with this affair that in a
little while **it issued in** joyful peace. It changed
the name of that place to Salem. The English
residents now numbered about " fiftie or sixtie per-
sons." Vast woods towered around them in lofty
and unbroken colonnades. But Endicott was built
for a pioneer. His stalwart arm laid low many a
monarch of the primeval trees, and his hearty voice
cheered on his men as they advanced into the
unknown gloom. They cut out roadways, built
bridges across the streams, and cleared off the
virgin soil, till, in the quaint language of the day,
. " they began to sett up ploughing."

Early letters were **sent** to England, where the
chartered company still remained ; Endicott being
the only original patentee who had come to America.
The patent of the Company of Massachusetts Bay
included all that part of New England stretching
from three miles north of the Merrimack to three
miles south of the Charles River, and " from the
Atlantic to the Pacific Ocean." " The Planter's
Plea," printed in 1630, speaking **of** these early let-
ters, says, " The good report of Capt. Endicott's
government, and the increase of the colony, began
to awaken the spirits of some persons not formerly

engaged." They were so "awakened," that, in June
of the same year, the whole company with its court
and charter transferred itself to the New World.
This was "the great arrival," amounting, altogether,
to "eleven shipps" and fifteen hundred souls.

Gov. Winthrop, by appointment from England,
superseded Gov. Endicott. We do not hear from
him one murmur of complaint at the loss of his
well-earned honors. He might have pointed to
the records of the Court, which testified, that "in
consideration of his meritt, worth, and good desert
— by erreccon of hands," he had been confirmed
in his office once and again. He might have recalled those two lone years of wise and valiant toil
for which Dr. Bentley says, that, " above all others,
he deserves the name of the Father of New England." But not a lisp of this is uttered. The first
governor of Massachusetts could obey as well as
command ; and, through all the administration of
his gifted and saintly rival, he was his firm support-
er and most sympathizing friend. Winthrop died
in 1649 ; and from that time, until his own death in
1665, Endicott was at the head of affairs. He
held the highest office in the Commonwealth for
sixteen different years, — a longer period than any
other governor under the original charter.

During the more retired portion of his life, he cultivated with great enthusiasm and taste his " Orchard Farm." The farm was situated three miles from Salem Town. It became after a few years the most beautiful spot in America. On three sides, its sunny slopes descended to the waves of the Atlantic. The mansion-house crowned a little eminence near by. That was the home of hospitality and love. By the most diligent inquiry we cannot find that there was ever any discord in the family. As an historical fact, the eldest son John cherished a filial and submissive spirit. He married Elizabeth Howchin, and would have courted only a pretty fancy had he doted on Edith Christison. The lord of our manor dwelt with dignity on his elegant estate. He used to make his journeys to and fro always by water. From the point at which he fastened his shallop, an avenue, overhung with plum-trees and grape-vines, led up to his very door. He was a leader in the agriculture of the colony. One time, he was tardy at the General Court. The excuse he forwarded was this, " He could not come up until the corne be sett." In 1648, he sold to William Trask five hundred apple-trees for two hundred acres of land ! In his will, dated 1650, he says, " I give to my

dear and loving wife Elizabeth all **my farm called**
'Orchard,' and yᵉ orchards, nurseries, fruit-trees,
gardens, and fences thereunto pertaining." **The**
traces of his labor **here** have disappeared. But one
venerable pear-tree, which he planted with his **own**
hand two hundred years ago, still **battles the storms**
of winter, and greets the gentler **gales of** summer.
It is a monument to his horticultural **zeal.**

Before Endicott had emigrated to **America, he**
bore the title of captain.   He was a soldier **to the**
end of his life.   He **was early** appointed Major-
general of the military forces in all the plantation. Those prompt, stern ways which **in after-**
years he carried **too** far, perhaps, into **the** civil
affairs he administered, were acquired in the midst
of arms, and on the perilous edge of battle.   One
renowned event must not be forgotten.   The royal
banner used by the colonial troops bore upon its
folds the crimson cross of St. George.   **It was a**
relic of papal idolatry.   The Puritan warrior could
not brook it.   And one day before they started on
an expedition, with his own keen sword he cut it
out bodily.   This daring act drew upon him the
wrath of the king.   Says a careful author, " It was
the first blow struck in America in defiance of the
royalty of England."   It would have cost **him his**

life had it not **been for the thunders** of rebellion **at home, which at that** time burst upon the head of Charles **the First.** All the chief men of the colony agreed in feeling with Endicott ; " the only difference being," says Mr. Felt, " that he manifested **his** opinion in deed, while they retained theirs in **secret."** The trusty blade with which this memora-**ble** deed was done is still preserved as a fine heirloom among his descendants.

Mr. Endicott **" was a** very virtuous gentleman," are the neat words **of the** annalist of that day, "and greatly beloved **of the most** as he well deserved." He was a rigorous magistrate ; but, as he **venerated justice with** his whole soul, he was certainly **a good one.** "**God** sifted a whole nation, that he might send choise **grain over** into this wilderness." **Was there** a choicer spirit that his ? He **came to** America from the impulse of heartfelt religion. " Whatever may have been the object of others," is the claim of his biographer, " there can be no doubt that *his* was the establishment of **a** church where he might enjoy Christ and his ordinances in their primitive purity." The poet of the company wrote for him this rare God-speed : —

" Strong, valiant John, wilt thou march on, and take up station **first ?**
    Christ called hath thee : his souldier be, and faile not of thy
    trust."

" Upon the account of religion," says the " Plea,"
the whole company sought an asylum here, " where
they could enjoy the liberty of their own persuasion, without disturbing the peace of the kingdom,
and without offence to others not like-minded with
themselves." Their hearts glowed with the hope
of planting a pure gospel amid the silent groves
of America. The first official letters from Matthew
Cradock, president of the Company in England,
to Endicott, then just " setting his corne," in the
little glades of the woods, contained this admonition,
" We trust you will not be unmindful of the *main
end* of our plantation, by endeavoring to bring the
Indians to the knowledge of the gospel." Among
the articles voted " to provide to send for New
England " are, " Ministers, the Patent under seal, a
Seal, Men skilled in making of pitch, of salt," &c.
The seal of the colony was an Indian, standing
erect, with an arrow in his right hand, encircled
with the motto, " Come over and help us." If any
of the " salvages " claimed a right to the land,
" they were to purchase their tytle, that they
might avoid the least scruple of intrusion." The
Puritans resorted to every expedient, that, with in-
defeasible, honor they might make " the holy experiment."

And ministers were sent, men of renown. A
church was formed in Salem, Aug. 6, 1629, — the
first church formed in America, the Plymouth
church having crossed the ocean ready-made. **Mr.**
Endicott's early pastor and spiritual father, Rev.
Mr. Skelton, became "teacher." The company
that sailed with Winthrop, after **barely** touching at
Salem, coasted along the curving bay for a more
commodious place. They **landed** on the north
bank of Charles River. **There** they decided to
build their homes, where now is the city of Charles-
town. By them a second church was constituted
July 30, **1630. But,** ere long, the beautiful penin-
sula of Shawmut allured them across the stream.
Nearly all moved thither ; and there they laid the
foundations **on which rapidly arose** the metropolis
of New England. **It** received the name of Boston, in honor of **the distinguished** John Cotton,
who came from Boston, England. For twenty-one
years, John Cotton had been vicar of St. Botolph's
Church, one of the most imposing cathedrals of
the realm. The lantern of its tower was two hundred and eighty feet above the ground, — a beacon
that could be seen by mariners far at sea. In consequence of this fact, St. Botolph was considered
the patron saint **of sailors.** It was said that "the

lamp there ceased to burn when Cotton **became a**
shining light in the wilderness of New England."
He exchanged the grandeur of such an edifice for
the pulpit of a little building in the woods, thatched
with straw, and walled with mud.   This original
structure stood on State Street, then King Street,
where now is the Merchants' Exchange.   In 1640,
it was replaced by a superior house, built of wood,
on the west side of Washington Street, not far
south of Court Street, then named Queen Street.
This was the church which afterwards resounded
with the sermons of John Norton and the outcries
of the Quakers.

   When Mr. Cotton, " the Nestor of New England," was on his death-bed, his despairing parish-
ioners implored him to name a successor.   He fell
into a troubled sleep : in it he dreamed that he saw
Mr. Norton of Ipswich, riding into Boston on a
snow-white horse. His waking thought he was convinced could be no better than **that.**   Mr. Norton
was his unfaltering appointment.   He was called
thereafter, " The falling mantle of the rising
prophet."   John Norton was a devoted preacher.
The maxim of his life was this, " Christ evidently
set forth is divine eloquence."   Yet he had to con-
tend with a " natural inclination to gayety ! "   He

was once addicted to excessive card-playing, but gave it up upon the admonition of a servant in his father's house. When at length he left his county in England, " an ancient man said he believed there was not more grace and excellence in all Essex than what Mr. Norton had carried away." The master of his college wished him to accept a fellowship in Cambridge, and his wealthy uncle desired to buy for him a valuable benefice ; but he declined them both for a simpler worship here. By nature he was a peacemaker. Through his kindly intervention, grave hostilities were prevented, that were likely to pass between " our people and the Dutch at Manhatoes " (Manhattan). At one time there was imminent danger of a break between the civil and religious orders. He preached, at a critical hour, the " Thursday Lecture ; " taking for his theme Ex. iv. 27, where Aaron met Moses in the mount, and kissed him. So clear and persuasive was his proof that there were reciprocal duties to be rendered, that the whole danger vanished at once, and harmony was restored to their councils. He was famed for his scholarship ; and his elegant Latin crossed the ocean again and again, in answer to knotty questions from Dutch and English divines.

" For he a rope of sand could twist
As tough as learned Sarbonist."

In the "Magnalia" of Cotton Mather, we read that "he had a neater style than most men; but he desired to furnish himself *ad pugnam,* rather than *ad pompam.*" Thomas Shepherd, his life-long friend, contrasted him with the schoolmen to their disadvantage.

> "Dull souls their tapers burn exceeding dim:
> They might to school again to learn of him."

He was reckoned by President Styles among the first quaternion of New England, "who were equal to the first characters in theology in all Christendom and in all ages." But, says a modern depictor, "his tenets surpassed in terror even those of the celebrated Calvin!" His temper was choleric; and, although it did not make him irascible, it gave a certain impetuosity to his thought, and led him to affirm that there were errors that could only be combated "with the holy tactics of the civil sword." But his most renowned gift was an unrivalled excellence in prayer. His whole soul seemed then to be aglow and aloft. Young divines used to resort to him as an example. So affluent and becoming were the holy thoughts he cherished, that sometimes for an hour together he continued his address to God, without weariness to himself or

those around him.   One aged man from Ipswich
used "ordinarially" to come on foot to Boston,
a distance of thirty miles, to be present at the
Thursday Lecture.   He said, "It was worth a
great journey to unite in one of Mr. Norton's
prayers."

And the influence of such lives as these pervaded
the Puritan community.   "I have lived," was the
testimony of Nathaniel Ward, the author of "The
Simple Cobbler of Agawam," "in a colony of many
thousand English, almost these twelve years, and
am held a very sociable man ; yet I may consid-
erately say I never heard but one oath sworn, nor
never saw one man drunk, in all that time."   A
book bearing the date 1643 affirms, "that one may
live there from year to year, and not see a drunkard,
or hear an oath, or meet a beggar."   "This remarkable private morality," thought Sir James
Mackintosh, "is worthy of attention, especially in
connection with the creeds they professed."   There
were, indeed, profane and sottish men, for there
were statute laws against them ; no stricter laws,
however, than there are to-day, than there ought to
be everywhere.   Education had already begun to
root itself in the soil of fair Harvard.   It was fos-
tered by care-taking hands.   Industry and trade

also flourished with the vigor of youth.   Their do-
minion over nature widened and improved.

> "Thus to men cast in that heroic mould
>   Came empire such as Spaniard never knew,
>   Such empire as beseems the just and true ;
>   And at the last, almost unsought, came gold."

This was the happy land,—John Endicott in the
chair of state, and John Norton in the leading pulpit, and Christian citizens in every post of duty,—
this was the land so soon to shudder beneath the
fatal tread of a dreadful mistake.

Religion and laws were closely intertwined in the
Puritan community: the government felt itself
bound to expatriate every disorderly person, as
much as the church was bound to excommunicate
him. They were like a household. They had
purchased their territory for a home. It was no
El Dorado : it was their Mount of Sion. With immense toil and unspeakable denials, they had
rescued it from the wild woods for the simple purpose that they might have a place for themselves
and their children to worship God undisturbed.
They knew nothing of toleration. They had not
thought of *that,* nor had the thought of it hardly
entered the world. Their right to shut the door

against intruders seemed to them as undoubted
and absolute as their right to breath the air around
them. The coming of the Quakers was to put the
validity of this right to a final test. At length it
was abandoned; but not until these devoted fields
had been the scene of the first tragedy of New
England.

The people called Quakers at the present day
possess in a high degree the respect of mankind.
They are known for the virtues of benevolence and
peace. Their little oddities of habit and speech
hardly provoke remark. The gentle spirits of Penn
and Barclay, the second founders of the sect, seem
to have passed into the entire body. They are mild
in their deportment, and leaders in every reform.
Clarkson and Hopper, Elizabeth Fry and John
Bright, are the foremost names in the philanthro-
pic movements of the age. There is one also,
dwelling on the banks of the Merrimack, whose calm
brow wears a chaplet woven by the shackled hands
of all the world. It crowns him also a true laureate
of America. He has not yet chosen for the
subject of his song the errors of his ancestry. But,
although such is their lofty excellence to-day, " seldom," says Palfrey, " have enthusiasts been more
coarse, more unfriendly, more wild and annoying,
than the early Friends."

There were, however, no excesses that could justify, even should they palliate, the cruelties with which they were received. Cotton Mather **said,** "If any man **will appear in** vindication of them, let him do as he **pleases ; for** my part I will **not."** It is to be noted **that the** more severe **laws against** them were passed **with great** difficulty, and, soon after the tumult in which they were executed, **were** regarded with universal regret. But the sole aim of them, we must remember, was to exclude the Quakers, and not to torment **them.** And says Mr. Bancroft, a great friend of the **sect,** " Prohibiting the arrival of Quakers was not persecution, and banishment is a term hardly to be used of one who has not acquired a home. When a pauper is sent to his native town, he is not called an exile." Now, the Puritans *disclaimed* the right to sit in judgment on the opinions of others. They denied that they persecuted for conscience' sake. " Non qua errones sed qua turbones," was the rule that they proclaimed. They believed that " hereticide was not an evangelical way for extinguishing heresies." Mr. Norton, the exponent of their **sterner** thoughts, himself asserted that neither Quakers nor others ought to be punished for their consciences ; that the law could take hold only of

their outward acts, and that only when they were
subversive of the good order **of the** land. And
brave old Roger Clap, commander of the Boston
Castle in 1665, wrote in his diary, concerning the
law that expelled Quakers from the jurisdiction on
pain of death, " The reason for that law was, because God's people could not worship the true and
living God in our public assemblies without being
disturbed by **them.** Some of them presumed to
return, to the loss of their lives for breaking
that law which was made **for our** peace and
safety."

Such was the plainly-uttered theory of their
proceedings. They committed their woful error
in the misjudgment of facts. Their fears were
overdrawn. They magnified eccentricities into
crimes, and regarded what was simply annoying as
a solemn danger. In the riot of swift events, their
practice often outran their principles ; and, in the
firm belief that New England was a theocracy,
they were not guiltless of the very wrongs from
which they had fled.

The first notice of the Quakers in Massachusetts
was an order of **the General** Court of 1656, appointing a "publick day of humiliation to seek the
face of God — in behalf of our native country, with

reference to the abounding of errors, especially those of the Ranters and Quakers." Hardly was the day passed when a vessel from Barbadoes, "The Swallow," Simon Kempthorn captain, arrived in "the Road before Boston," with two Quaker women on board, — Ann Austin and Mary Fisher. Officers visited the vessel, and, searching their trunks, found about a hundred Quaker books. The Council thereupon, "tendering the preservation of the peace and truth," did order, —

First, that all such corrupt books be burned in the market-place by the common executioner.

Second, that the said Ann and Mary be kept in close prison until such time as they be transferred out of the country.

Third, that the said Simon Kempthorn is enjoined to transport, or cause to be transported, the said persons from hence to Barbadoes, from whence they came ; and, for the more effectual performance thereof, he is to give security in a bond of one hundred pounds sterling.

While **they were in jail, a** board was nailed up before the window, that no one might hold communication with them. Nicholas Upsall, an aged citizen, was deeply interested in their behalf, and purchased food for them every week, "lest they

should **be starved.**" After five weeks' confinement, they re-embarked for Barbadoes.

The maiden Mary continued her romantic travels.
"Being moved of the Lord" to deliver a message
to the Sultan of Turkey, she entered upon a journey towards the Sublime Porte. She toiled along by
land from the coasts of Morea to the city of Adrianople. This part of her journey, about six hundred miles, she made alone, "without abuse or in-
jury." At Adrianople, she found the grand vizier
encamped with all his **army.** She discovered means
of announcing her arrival, which was done in these
words: "An English woman hath a message from
the great God to the great Turk." She was soon
invited to his tent, and with the aid of three inter-
preters "uttered her mind." He listened "with
much gravity and soberness," and offered her a
guard for her further progress. She declined it,
and departed for Constantinople alone, "whitherto
she came without the least hurt or scoff." In
George Bishope's book, which was published
in 1661, with the title, "New England judged
by the Spirit of the Lord," Mary was said to
fare better among the heathens than among the
Christians, "to the glory of the great Turk, and
his great renown, and your everlasting shame and

contempt!" **The** Orientals regarded lunatics as **inspired**: therefore they overwhelmed the Quakers with prodigious quantities of genuflections **and** salams. They bowed them **out** of the country, never to be troubled by them again.

No sooner had these two unwelcome visitors departed than another vessel, sailing from London, brought eight more Quakers to our inhospitable shore. Their treatment was similar to that of the first party. After eleven weeks of **suffering in the** jail, they embarked again "for no place but England." Their behavior was said **to be** "uncivil." Mary Prince shouted out **a malediction upon the** governor as he **was going by the** prison from his place of worship: she also wrote him a letter "filled with opprobrious stuff." The governor sent for her to come to his own house. He had invited two ministers to be present, and, "with much tenderness," they endeavored to induce her to desist from her extravagances. To this exhortation she returned the grossest reproaches, calling them "hirelings, deceivers of the people, Baal's priests, the seed of the serpent," &c. Such, it appears, was their usual style of addressing all rulers in State and Church.

Thus far, action against the Quakers had pro-

3

ceeded upon the general **law** against heresy. The
emergency seemed to require some special legislation. **The** Federal Commissioners at their annual
meeting, Sept. 17, 1656, recommended such legisla-
tion to the four United Colonies. The General
Court of Massachusetts promptly acted in the
matter. On the 14th **of October,** the first law was
passed against the Quakers. **They** are called " a
cursed sect, who take upon them to speak and write
blasphemous opinions, despising governments,
reviling magistrates **and ministers,** and seeking to
turn the people to their pernicious ways." The
law forbade " the master of any ship, bark, pink, or
catch," to bring Quakers " into any harbour, creek,
or cove of the jurisdiction," upon pain of a hun-
dred pounds' fine. It **prohibited the** Quakers
themselves from coming on **pain of** immediate
imprisonment and severe castigation. Such was
the excitement into which the government had been
thrown by the events **of** the summer, that this law
was published in the market-place, and through the
streets of Boston, by beat of the drum. When it
was proclaimed at the door of Nicholas Upsall,
" the good old man," says Joseph Besse in his
" Sufferings of the Quakers," published in 1753,
" grieved in spirit, publically testified against it,"

demanding "that they take heed what they did,
lest they be found fighters against God." This
was considered seditious language; and poor
Upsall, who had before been excommunicated
from the Church, was now fined twenty pounds,
and ordered to leave the country within a
month. His fine was partly abated at the request of his wife, and he was permitted to stay in
Sandwich until the rigor of winter was passed. He
then was welcomed " to a warm house " by an Indian prince in Rhode Island. In three years, he
returned from his exile, and, refusing to retract his
offensive speeches, he was again remanded to the
Boston prison. After being there two years, " he
drew so many persons to him," that he was transferred to the Castle. Soon, however, permission
was granted him to dwell with his brother in Dor-
chester, "provided he do not corrupt any with his
pernicious opinions." This was the end of his sad
persecutions, and here he ended his stormy life in
an eventide of comparative peace.

But the new law was not to be a dead letter.
The next year, 1657, Mary Clark left her husband
and six children in London, and sailed across the
Atlantic, " that she might warn these persecutors to
desist from their iniquity." She delivers her mes-

sage, is scourged, and committed to prison for twelve weeks. She is then sent away. Christopher Holder, one of the eight who had been reshipped to England, appeared again in Salem, and "spoke a few words in meeting after the priest had done." This "speaking a few words in meeting" we shall find hereafter, was a most startling disturbance to the solemn Puritans. George Fox, previous to this, when a Rev. doctor had preached upon the theme, "Ho! every one that thirsteth, come ye, buy without money and without price," was "moved of the Lord" to cry out, "Come down, thou deceiver: dost thou bid people to come to the waters of life freely, and yet thou takest three hundred pounds a year of them?" In the Salem church, Holder was "haled back by the hair of his head, and his mouth violently stopped with a glove and handkerchief thrust thereinto." The next day he was "had to Boston." He received thirty stripes, and the jailer's custody for nine weeks. He continued to disturb public worship in various places, suffering repeated imprisonments, and at length the loss of his right ear.

The law of 1656 checked the influx of Quakers, but did not stop it entirely. It was amended Oct. 14, 1657, to this effect: "Every one who know-

ingly entertained a Quaker should pay forty shil-
lings for each hour of hospitality. Quaker men,
if they returned after the first expulsion, should
have one ear cut off; if they returned again, they
should lose the other. Quaker women, in each
case, were to be severely whipped ; and for every
Quaker, he or she, that should a third time herein
again offend, they should have their tongues thrust
through with a hot iron." The first of these muti-
lations was inflicted in three instances only, the
others not at all.

The populace murmured against such inhumani-
ties. They were thrown into a tumult of rebellion
when the story of a strange outrage burst forth from
the prison-walls. One William Brend, said "to be
of a turbulent spirit, and forward to abuse men
with his tongue," had addressed this communication to the magistrates : " The Lord of this Campe,
whom ye world derides, persecutes, and in scorne
calls Quakers, will by them dash ye nations to
pieces ; therefore repent — for opposing ye Lord
in any of his servants by fines, imprisonments, and
banishments. This is a message sent from ye
most high God of heaven and earth into New England ; though you will not believe it, you shall
know it." This poor enthusiast, according to

Quaker **authorities, endured** terrific abuses from
the "inhumane **gaoler." Though** "a man in years,
he **put him** in **irons,** neck and heels so close
together that there was no more room left between
each than for the lock that fastened them." Thus
he kept him from five in the morning till after nine
at night, "being the space of sixteen hours." The
next morning, he brought him **to the mill** to work.
Brend refused, "having been kept five days without eating, and unmercifully beaten with a rope."
Then **the** "butcherly fellow " "**began to** beat anew,
and laid fourscore and seventeen more blows on
him ;" **so** that his back and arms were bruised and
black. "**His whole** flesh had become a jelly,"
and "**his** senses **were** stopped." ·He would have
died, "had it not pleased God miraculously to heal
him." The **noise of** such brutality flew through
the town. The governor sent his own surgeon to
the prison **to** afford what aid he could ; and **the**
magistrates — for they feared a mutiny — "set up
a paper on the meeting-house door, and up and
down the streets," declaring their abhorrence of
the outrage, and **promising to** punish the jailer.
"But," **says Besse,** "this paper was soon taken
down **at the** instigation of the high priest, John
Norton, who did not stick to say, 'William Brend

endeavoured to beat our gospel ordinances black
and blue; if *he* then be beaten black and blue, it
is but just upon him; and I will appear in his
behalf that did so.'"

Under the presidency of Endicott, the Federal
commissioners met again in Boston, in 1658. It
was this session which propounded to the several
courts their most sanguinary laws. When the
court of Massachusetts met, a memorial was presented by twenty-four citizens, praying for the legislation they proposed. They quoted the example
of other Christian states; referred to the ineffect-
ual remedies hitherto employed; announced the
principle of *se defendendo;* and, finally, put the
question, "whether it be not necessary," if Quakers continue to obtrude themselves, "to punish so
high incorrigibleness in such and so many capital
evils with death."

The provision of a threat of death against banished persons had been the resort of Massachusetts
through a long course of years. It had heretofore
never once failed of its object. "There can be
no doubt," says Palfrey, "that among those who
favored this new enactment, there was a confi-
dent persuasion that the terror of the law would
accomplish all that was desired, and would pre-

vent any occasion for its execution." — " The object of this severity," says Bancroft, " was not to
persecute, but to exclude them."

On the 20th of October, their most extreme
measure was adopted. Thenceforward, persons
convicted by special jury of belonging to "the pernicious sect of Quakers should be sentenced to
banishment, on pain of death."

The House which passed this implacable act
consisted of twenty-five members. When it was
first put to vote, it was promptly rejected. Upon
a motion to reconsider, a long and excited debate
ensued. At length, it was carried in the affirma-
tive, by a vote of thirteen to twelve. One voice
was wanting to avert the calamity. This fact so
troubled good Deacon Wozel, who was absent because of illness, that " he got to the court weeping
for grief," and said, " If he had not been able to
go [walk], he would have crept upon his knees
rather than such a law should pass."

The government had crossed the Rubicon. It had
taken a position which it could not abandon without humiliation, or maintain without cruelty. The
court seemed in some degree sensible of the import of their act. In deference to the public sentiment opposing them, they voted that a paper be

composed and printed "to manifest the evil of the tenets of the Quakers, and the danger of their practices." This business was assigned to " John Norton, Teacher, of Boston." It was published at the public charge, and bore the title, " The Heart of New England Rent at the Blasphemies of the Present Generation ; or, A brief Tractate concerning the **Doctrine** of the Quakers," — " which doctrine," says Cotton Mather, " was in this tract solidly confuted ; and perhaps it had been better if this had been all the confutation, which I add because I will not — I cannot — make myself a vindicator of the severities that followed."

But desperate souls were abroad, men who looked upon this menace as an invitation, and sprang forward at once to avail themselves of the chance of martyrdom. Marmaduke Stevenson, a young man then in Barbadoes, heard of the " bloody **law**," and took passage immediately for New England. He reached Rhode Island, and found there his friend, William Robinson, to whom, in the language of a letter from the cell in which he lay condemned to die, " **the** word of the Lord had come expressly, and commanded me to pass to the town **of Bos**-ton, my life to lay down." — " After a little time," **as** a similar letter asserted, " the word of the

Lord came to Marmaduke also, saying, 'Go to Boston with thy brother, William Robinson." The two accordingly went. Mary Dyer, "a comely, grave woman, the mother of several children," likewise was "moved of the Lord to come from Rhode Island to make them a visit." Nicholas Davis also was one of the party. A delicate little girl, only eleven years old, thrilled with the fine enthusiasm, came all the way "from her father's house in Providence to bear witness against your persecuting spirit." The court decided that she was too young for trial ; and a sturdy, kind-hearted judge agreed to carry her safely home. The four others were arrested, and straightway banished, on pain of death. Nicholas and Mary "found freedome to depart ;" but the other two were "constrained in the love and power of the Lord to try your bloody law unto death." They hovered about Salem a few weeks, and then, in the midst of quite a troop of Friends, marched into Boston with unfaltering steps. They reversed the precept of the Master, "When they shall persecute you in one city, flee ye into another." They certainly courted the fatal event. Alice Cowland, one who came with them, brought some "linnen," as she showed the governor, "wherein to wrap the dead bodies

of them who were to suffer." Mary Dyer recon-
sidered her duty, and was also "soon espied" in
Boston.

Here, then, were three heroic fanatics, who had
committed a mortal offence. It was done with the
clear intention of defying a statute-law. What
ought to be the course of the makers of that law,
when driven to such an extremity? Drop it at
once, we say; cast off your rash enactment; forbid
the suicide; let no judgment convert a mad-cap
into a martyr's crown. Possibly the invaders expected this victory in the final encounter. Better,
far better, that they had obtained it, than that one
life should be lost in a mere contest of excited
wills!

But those iron men with whom they dealt knew
not how to bend. The government felt that it
could not yield. John Endicott said to them in
the open court, "We have made many laws to keep
you from amongst us. I do not desire your death."
He briefly reverted to the danger they brought to
their peace-loving State, and then, "speaking
faintly," says Bishope, "as a man whose life was
departing from him," pronounced the sentence,
"You shall be had back to the place from whence
you came, and from thence to the place of execu-

tion, to be hanged **on the gallows** till you are dead."

The 27th of October, 1659, **is a dark day** in the calendar of New England. As the afternoon began to decline, these three persons, "led by the back **way,"** because they "were afraid of the fore way, lest it should affect the people too much;" guarded **by a** band of two hundred men, armed with halberds, **and by a troop of horse, with** drums beating to drown whatever they might say; "walking hand in hand, Mary being the middlemost," — took up their solemn march to the gallows. It stood upon Boston Common, perhaps beneath the Great Elm. **The two men,** one after the other, climbed the ladder, **and were hanged. They** died with exalted **hearts. The last** words **of** Robinson were, "I suffer **for Christ, in** whom **I live, and for** whom I die." Stevenson said, "This **day** shall we **be** at rest with the Lord." Mary Dyer then stepped up the **ladder. The halter was put about her neck; her face was covered with a handkerchief; she was just to be turned off, — when a **faint** cry arrested the **hangman's act.** It was **this:** "Stop! stop! she **is reprieved!"** "A reprieve! a reprieve!" was shouted back and forth by a hundred willing voices. The **execution** immediately stopped. But she,

whose mind was already, as it were, in heaven,
stood still, and said, " she was there willing to suffer as her brethren did, unless they would annul
their wicked law."   Could there be a deeper pathos
than that ?   Her own son, who was secretary of
state in Rhode Island, had come to Boston to in-
tercede in her behalf.   The magistrates could not
refuse him ; and he bore his dauntless mother back
to their home.

At this point, the resentment and compassion of
the people overleaped all restraint, and burst out in
ominous threats.   The court, still sitting, felt com-
pelled to justify their action.   Two declarations
were drawn up, — one to be printed, and the other
to be sent to the several towns.   They are preserved in the Massachusetts Records.   They plead
the cause of the judges in these words : " Altho'
the justice of our proceedings against William
Robinson, Marmaduke Stevenson, and Mary Dyer,
supported by the authority of this court, and the
laws of the country, and the laws of God, may
rather persuade us to expect encouragement and
commendation from all prudent and pious men,
than convince us of any necessity to apologize for
the same, yet, forasmuch as men of weaker parts,
out of pity and commiseration (a commendable

4

and Christian virtue, **yet easily** abused, and susceptible of sinister and dangerous impressions), for **want** of full information, may be less satisfied, and **men of** perverse principles may take occasion **hereby** to calumniate us, and render us bloody persecutors, — **to satisfy** the one, and stop the mouth of the other, we thought it requisite to declare, that, about three years since, divers persons professing **themselves to be Quakers . . .** arrived in Boston, whose persons were only secured to be sent away **by** the first opportunity without censure or punishment, although their design was to undermine and **ruin . . .** the peace and order here established. Accordingly, a law was made prohibiting **Quakers from coming into this** jurisdiction on penalty of the house of correction till they be sent away. Notwithstanding **which, by a** back door, **they found entrance ; . . . the penalty** was therefore increased : which also being too weak a defence **against their** impetuous and fanatic fury, a law was made, that such persons should be banished on **pain** of death, according to the example of England **in their provision** against Jesuits. . . . The consideration **of our** gradual proceedings will vindicate us **from** the clamorous accusation of severity, our own **just and necessary defence calling upon** us (other measures failing) to offer the points which these persons have violently and wilfully rushed upon, and thereby are become *felons de se*, which might have been prevented, **and the sovereign** law, *salus populi*, been preserved.   **Our former** proceedings, as well as the sparing of Mary **Dyer** upon an inconsiderable intercession, will manifestly evince that we desire their *life absent* rather than their *death present*."

The second document **also reviews their legisla**tion, and then presents the following reasons for insisting upon the extreme penalty :—

1st. **The doctrine of the sect destroys** the fundamental truths **of religion.**

2d. They renounce openly **the** command of God to obey magistrates.

3d. If death may be lawfully exacted for breach of confinement, it certainly may for breach of **banishment.**

4th. As a householder may repel an intruder with the **sword,** so may a government.

5th. A parent defends his family against a pestiferous visitor : thus should rulers defend their subjects against moral contagion.

6th. This is not the persecution of Christians ; for Christians, when **persecuted in** one city, flee into another.

This twofold **plea went forth** to the people.   **It**
was thoughtfully drawn, and indicated truly that
the court was not impelled alone by either
eyeless bigotry or mad vexation. Probably it
convinced some of the disaffected : no doubt it was
thoroughly believed by the upright men who pro-
claimed it. Authorities in jurisprudence of the
present day have testified that " they had upon their
side that sort of rigid justice which proceeds upon
the established rule that a *perfect right* may be
maintained at *any cost* to the invader." But, in
answer to such a proposition, our hearts affirm that
life is too precious a thing to be trampled upon by
the heel of meagre consistency, and humanity ought
never to be surrendered **to a** principle of logic.
Defeat in such conditions would have been more
noble than success.

In the mellowed light of history, with reference
to this entire contention, we can all see the truthful-
ness of those ancient verses of the " Simple Cobbler
of Agawam : "—

> " They seldom lose the **field, but often win,**
>   **That end their** wars before **their wars** begin."

Mary Dyer could not be at rest.   The next spring
" **she was moved to return** to the bloody town of Bos-

ton." Her husband wrote beseechingly to Endicott, that he had not seen her above this half-year; that she had journeyed secretly and speedily all about, and at length had come to Boston. " Unhappy journey, may I say, and woe to that generation that help one another to hazard their lives, for I know not what end, and to what purpose ! "

Endicott was loath to condemn her. He even crossed his nature enough to suggest to her the evasion of denying her identity. There had been another Mrs. Dyer in the Province. But she would not equivocate. With wonderful heroism she marched to her fate. When her sentence was pronounced upon her, she replied, " I came in obedience to the will of God ; the last General Court desiring you to repeal your unrighteous laws, and that same is my work now, and earnest request." On the morning of the next day, she was led forth a second time to the place of execution. They were anxious to save her. Even at the gallows they delayed the execution ; and her life was offered her again and again, if she would only promise to leave the jurisdiction. " Nay, I cannot," was her constant reply ; for " in obedience to the will of the Lord I came, and in his will I abide faithful to death."

4*

There was but one more victim of this direful
enactment. A resident of Barbadoes, named
William Leddra, after repeated disturbances in
Salem and Newbury, and corresponding chastise-
ments, upon his third return in 1661 was brought to
trial and doomed to the gallows. He was charged
him with contempt for authorities, because he refused to remove his hat, and for saying "thee" and
"thou." His reply was, "Will you put me to death
for speaking good English, and for not putting off
my clothes?" — "A man may speak treason in good
English," was the sharp response. "Will you return
to England?" they demanded. "I have no business there," he said. Simon Bradstreet pointed a
menacing finger to the scaffold, saying, "Then you
shall go there." — "Will you put me to death for
breathing the air of your jurisdiction? I appeal to
the laws of England." Says Mr. Chandler in his
"American Criminal Trials," "Twenty years before it had been accounted perjury and treason
to speak of appeals to the king." Yet, after this,
he was offered his life if he would promise to
leave the Province. Still refusing, he was con-
signed to his fate. He wrote to his friends from
his prison-cell, the day before his death, a letter
full of pure and charming sentiment. "The sweet

influences of the morning star, distilling into my innocent habitation, have so filled me with the joy of
the Lord, in the beauty of holiness, that my spirit
is as if it did not inhabit a tabernacle of clay, but is
wholly swallowed up in the bosom of eternity."
He took tender leave of his fellow-captives, and
went to the gallows in a gentle and saintly way.
A stranger in the crowd, just arrived by sea, was
smitten with overwhelming pity. He cried out,
"For God's sake, take not away the man's life, but
remember Gamaliel's counsel to the Jews." The
captain of the guard bade him hold his peace, and
he departed in tears. "All that will be Christ's
disciples must take up the cross," Leddra murmured at the foot of the ladder. His last words
were the prayer of lofty resignation, — "Lord
Jesus, receive my spirit."

At the height of Leddra's trial, Wenlock Christison, another of the banished, suddenly strode into
the court, and took his stand by the side of the
prisoner. His appearance sent dismay into the
the minds of the judges. He confronted them
with wild and dreadful words. "Are not you the
man who was banished on pain of death?" demanded Endicott, in a troubled voice. "Yea, I
am," was the deep-toned reply. "What dost thou

here, then?" he said. "I come to warn you that
you shed no **more innocent blood ;** for the blood
that you have shed cries to the Lord **God** for vengeance to come upon you." Endicott was weary
enough of that bloody **work ;** and here was another
victim madly rushing to the altar. Christison had
suffered much before this for his obstinate turbu-
lence. It was thought that at length he had been
effectually dismissed. They committed him once
again.

After three months, when he was brought to trial,
a great change **had come over the court.** At the
beginning **of** that period, they would have passed
sentence **upon him at** once, without disagreement :
now they contested the point for more than two
weeks. The governor was vexed at what he
thought their lack **of** nerve. Hurling something
violently upon the table, he said, "I could find it in
my heart to go home [to England] ; I thank God I
am not afraid to give judgment." Would that he
had been afraid ! The metal of his nature was the
stuff of which martyrs are made : it was not tem-
pered enough for a martyr's judge.

A majority was at length obtained for the condemnation, " provided, nevertheless, that if the said
Christison shall at any time before the execution,

by writing under his hand, engage that he forthwith depart this jurisdiction, **and from** thenceforth return no more into it, without having first obtained leave from the General Court or Council, he shall thereupon be discharged." In the Massachusetts Archives may be found this letter : —

I the condemned man doe give **forth** under my hand that if I may **have** my libarty, I have freedome to depart this Jurisdiction, and I know not y^t ever I shall **com** into it **any more.**

WINLOCK CHRISTISON.

from ye goal in Boston,
ye 7th day of ye 4th mo. 1661.

But there were signs that the fury of the conflict was nearly spent, that the wild **tide** of fanaticism had begun to turn. Strong wills had been pitted against each other in a desperate encounter. The Quaker had conquered. His gallant fortitude could not be overawed. The chief men of Boston saw, with astonishment and horror, the dreaded sect increase just in proportion to the number and severity of the laws against them. Said **Christison at his trial,** "There came five in place of the last **man** you executed." The authorities were wholly disarmed when even the threat of death, instead of a weapon to repel, proved a magnet to draw them.

With such indomitable audacity they had no power
to cope.

When the court assembled on the 22d of May,
the Quakers had assumed the offensive. In the
diary of a private citizen, under this date may be
found this significant entry: "The Quakers have
given out such speeches as gave cause to think they
intended mischief unto our magistrates and ministers, and threatened fire and sword to be our speedy
portion!"

The feeling of compassion also, which all along
had muttered among the people its growing dissent,
now rose in overpowering rebukes. These voices
could not be longer braved. This court, therefore,
persuaded by such means, though it could not bring
itself at once to a full repeal of its law for capital
punishment, enacted an amendment which it well
knew would supersede its execution. "Being desi-
rous to try all means, with as much lenity as may
consist with our safety, to prevent the intrusion of
the Quakers, who, besides absurd and blasphemous
doctrines, like rogues and vagabonds come among
us" [thus shifting their ground of legislation from
that of heresy to that of vagrancy], "the Court has
ordered that every such vagabond Quaker," ad-
judged to be "one that hath not any dwelling or

orderly allowance as an inhabitant of this jurisdiction, shall be stripped naked from the middle up-
wards, and tied to a cart's tail, and whipped through
the town," — and so on "till they be conveyed
through any of the outmost towns of our Jurisdiction." Should they return after being three times
thus dealt with, they shall be branded with the letter
R on their left shoulder, whipped, and sent away
again ; "and," it is added in compliment to their
dishonored past, should they return yet again, they
are to be made amenable to "the law made anno
1658 for their banishment on pain of death."

No hanging or branding ever took place in consequence of this legislation.

It has been commonly maintained that a man-
date from Charles II. put a stop to the ill treatment
of Quakers in New England, and that his royal intervention alone saved them from utter destruction.
This opinion Mr. Palfrey confutes. Several months
before his gracious order crossed the sea, our
harsher laws had been mollified, and the resolution
fully taken to put no more of them to death. The
proud magistrates, however, were quite willing to
have the king's injunction generally regarded as
the *motive* for the new indulgences rather than any
change of judgment on their part. They were more

stiff than cruel; and it was easier to bow to the sov-
ereignty of Charles than bend to the confession of
a mistake.   And in one view the royal will just ac-
corded with their own: it removed the very men
they were most anxious to be rid of.   No doubt it
hastened, and also widened, the returning tide of
good feeling.

Four months before it came, under the new law
all the Quakers in prison, twenty-seven in number,
were released, and sent out of the jurisdiction without punishment.   Many of these had come into
Boston clad in sackcloth and ashes, pronouncing
tremendous woes upon the bloody city.

As the clemency of the rulers began its gentler
sway, for a time at least the vehemence of the disturbers seemed to increase.   Their antics became
even more grotesque than before.   George Wilson,
one of those first released, paced slowly through
the streets of Boston, crying with a loud voice,
"The Lord is coming forth with fire and sword to
plead with this city."   Elizabeth Hooton, an aged
English woman, who had been severely whipped
three or four times, delivered a similar message in
the streets of Cambridge.

But their favorite place of denouncing was "the
steeple-house;" and their favorite victim was

"the man-made minister." **The early Puritans** had a sacred love for their public worship, **and a** peculiar reverence for the preacher of righteousness. Imagine the horror occasioned by such a scene as this. Four women arrive from Barbadoes on the Lord's day. Mary Brewster is their leader. She hurries **with** them to the door of the South Church. There, casting off her shoes and riding-suit, with hair dishevelled and streaming over her **shoulder, in a long robe of sackcloth whose** ragged edge frets her bare feet, **with her face be-**grimed with grease and lampblack, she rushes **into** the midst of the silent congregation, and, in a quaking voice, announces herself as "a Sign of the Black Pox," which was soon to appear in judgment upon them! She afterwards confessed, that, three years before, this service was laid upon her of the Lord, and that her husband was willing for her to perform it! Simon Bradstreet, in his warrant, calls their offence "the making an horrible disturbance on the Lord's day, and affrighting the people of **the** South Church in Boston in the time of the publick dispensation **of the** word." The constable could **not identify her when she** was brought before the court ; for he says, "She was then in the shape of the Devil." Owning herself to be the culprit, however, she was whipped "up and down the town with twenty lashes."

During another service, Thomas Newhouse stalked into the broad aisle of the church with two great glass bottles in his hands, and, gloomily turning about, in the face of the whole congregation broke them one against the other, proclaiming in a prophetic manner, "Thus will the Lord break you in pieces."

Lydia Wardell, "being a young and tender and chaste woman," in obedience to the inward light, as a sign of the spiritual nakedness of her neighbors, with the encouragement of her husband, " though it was exceeding hard to her modest and shamefaced disposition," went into the crowded church without a shred of clothing upon her. Deborah Wilson, " a young woman of very modest and retired life, and of sober conversation, as were her parents," was constrained " to go through the town of Salem " in a similar plight, " as a sign."

The Quaker author, Besse, though writing many years after the excitement of the day, approves these displays, and applauds the poor dupes who made them. Is it strange, however, that the guardians of public morals should seek to repress them, even by the whips of justice? It is related by Gra-

hame, that one man, named Faubord, undertaking
to imitate Abraham, was really about to offer up
his son as a sacrifice ; his neighbors, hearing the
cries of the lad, broke into his house just in time
to prevent the blasphemous atrocity.

But in general, it must be allowed, the absurdity
of their behavior was harmless. They were pure
and lovable in their private lives ; and their public
pranks even were free from guile. There was an
"inward light." It shed its gentle radiance over acts
that would be otherwise dark indeed. It did not
cease to shine all through their lurid sufferings.
George Fox had converted his pillory into a pulpit ;
and he made so many converts of the gaping crowd
that gathered round it, that they liberated him " in a
tumultuous manner," and set a clergyman, who had
been instrumental in his punishment, in the very
position he had occupied. And so *they* preached
in the court and the prison, at the cart's tail, and
even on the ladder of death. Day and night an
increasing throng gathered about their places of
punishment. The Puritans ought to have learned
before this that persecution was one of the surest
means to propagate a religious persuasion.

The number of sufferers during the whole period
of these severities was comparatively small : it was

only about thirty. An address to the king, from the pen of a Quaker, before it was entirely ended, gave this summary: "Twenty-two have been banished upon pain of death, three have been martyred, three have had their right ears cut, one hath been burned in the hand with the letter H, thirty-one persons have received six hundred and fifty stripes, . . . one thousand and forty-four pounds worth of goods have been taken from them, and one now lieth in fetters, condemned to die." Edward Burrough, who probably wrote this address, at length obtained access to the royal ear. He spoke to his Majesty thus: "There is a vein of innocent blood opened in your dominions, which, if not stopped, may overrun all." Whereupon the king said, "I will stop that vein;" "not liking," as a student of his character has affirmed, the "annoyance of refusing a request."

A *mandamus* was at once prepared in these words: —

CHARLES R.

Trusty and well beloved, we greet you well. Having been informed that several of our subjects amongst you, called Quakers, have been and are imprisoned by you, whereof some have been executed, and others (as hath been represented unto us) are in danger to undergo the like: We have thought fit to signify our pleasure in that behalf for the future, and do hereby require, that if there be any of those people now amongst you, now already condemned to suffer death or other corporal punishment, or that are imprisoned, and obnoxious to the like condemnation, you are to forbear to proceed any further therein, but that you forthwith send the said persons, whether condemned or imprisoned, over into this Our Kingdom of England, together with the respective crimes or offenses laid to their charge, to the end such course may be taken with them here as shall be agreeable to our laws and their demerits ; and for so doing these our letters shall be your sufficient warrant and discharge.

Given at Our Court at Whitehall the ninth day of Sept., 1661, in the thirteenth year of Our Reign.

To Our trusty and well-beloved John Endicott, Esquire, &c.

By his Majesty's Command,

WILLIAM MORRIS.

Samuel Shattock, who had formerly been banished from Salem, was commissioned to convey this rescript to the Colony. A ship was at once chartered by a subscription among the Friends ; and Ralph Goldsmith, also a Friend, sailed as captain. After a voyage of six weeks, they arrived in Boston harbor. It was Sabbath day. Several citizens, seeing the English colors flying from the mast, at once came aboard, and inquired if they had any letters from England. "No, not to-day," replied Goldsmith, keeping close about the errand of de-

5*

liverance on which he came. Capt. Oliver, who had commanded the city forces during the excitement of the executions, was one of the visitors. "Supposing," says Bishope, "they were most Quakers, he came into Boston, and said, as is reported, 'There is Shattock, and the Devil and all!'"

The next morning, Capt. Goldsmith, with Samuel Shattock, the king's deputy, went on shore; and they two went directly through the town to the governor's house, on Pemberton Square, whither he had removed his official residence at the request of the court, "out of respect to strangers." They knocked at the door. He sent out a servant to know their business. They replied that their message was from the king of England, and they would deliver it to none but himself. "Then they were admitted to go in; and the governor came to them, and commanded Samuel Shattock's hat to be taken off. Having received the deputy and the *mandamus*, he laid off his own hat, ordering Shattock's hat to be given him again. He then went out into the street, and bade the two Friends follow him." After finding Deputy-Governor Bellingham, and consulting with him, he came back, and uttered the laconic speech, "We shall obey his Majesty's command!"

This utterance was decisive ; and the joyful officers hastened back to the vessel, and gave liberty
to the waiting passengers to come ashore. " Out
must the Quakers be put of the prisons ; " and
that night " they all met together, and offered up
praises to God for this wonderful deliverance."

Thus terminated, on the 25th of November, 1661,
the sufferings of the Quakers in America.   Later
than this, there were instances of extravagance on
the one hand, and violence on the other.   The
court, in a moment of anger, at one time revived
and re-affirmed the statute-law against them ; but
the penalties were more lightly inflicted, and soon
altogether ceased.   Several of the odd gambols
described above happened after the pressure of
persecution was removed.   Ere long, however,
they had also ceased.   In a few years, William
Penn, whose courtly grace had already named him
" The Quaker King," leaving the gaud and glory
of a palace came to the banks of the Delaware,
and erected a sylvan throne in the groves of the
West.   The effulgence of his example threw a
milder coloring over Quaker customs throughout
the world.

" It is a hard measure," says a learned barrister,
" to visit upon the colonists of New England the

sins of all Christendom." Intolerance was the mistake of the age. Every nation into which the Quaker came persecuted him with peculiar rigor. Of all new sects, the first appearance of this one was most offensive. Its attitude seemed insolent and dangerous. The Quaker denounced the existing worship as an abomination, and government everywhere as treason. Even Roger Williams, "The Apostle of Liberty," contended that there were bounds of civil order that must be preserved, and that the Quakers had certainly transgressed them. The Governor of Rhode Island, which was the " backe door " of their entrance to Massachusetts, admitted "that their doctrines tend to very absolute cutting down and overturning relations and civil government among men." He could not fight ; he could not swear ; he could not pay tithes.

> " Region, estate, rule civil and divine,
> Religion, — all they seek to undermine."

This was the feeling of affrighted men. Instead of the broad-brimmed and opulent gentleman, whose mild deportment calms and delights us in the feverish excitement of to-day, the vision then was a wild and dreamy-eyed fanatic, running up and down the earth propagating fatuitous doctrine,

and vilifying the most respected men.   Taken
with "mighty convincements," they invaded the
Vatican of the Pope, as well as the Kremlin of
the Czar.   They had "drawings" to the Moors
and the Tartars, and even to the Emperor of China.
And their idea of missions was as grotesque as
their journeys were romantic.   A mission was not
the sober inculcation of truth: it was a thunder-
clap of execration.   They would "deliver," and
then depart.   Such performances in our day would
have opened to them the door of asylums, rather
than shut upon them the door of jails.   "They
were," says Mather, "madmen, — a sort of luna-
ticks, dæmoniacks, and enurgumens."

Now, the Puritans knew no better how to treat
them than other men.   It certainly can be shown
that they did treat them no *worse.*

Besse gives the *names* of more than ten hundred
Quakers who suffered imprisonment, torture, scour-
ging, or transportation in England, and the *names* of
almost two hundred whose sufferings there ended
in death.   Does such a stupendous fact make it
becoming for the mother country to lay upon her
daughter the charge of special cruelty?   By an
Act of Parliament as late as 1662, Quakers were
subjected to a heavy fine for holding their meetings,

and, for a third offence, were to be transported to a distant colony. In consequence of this law, whole ship-loads were carried into exile. And the mob of England, — the very reverse of what was true in America, — in spite against the Quakers, used to hound on the magistrate, and redouble the punishment. In one case, the house in which they had met was torn down over their heads. They gathered upon the ruins : they could not be dispersed by armed men. And there, huddled close together on that woful pile, the rabble seized shovels to throw the rubbish over them. They were almost buried alive before they were driven off.

And shall we speak approvingly, even in contrast with our acknowledged fault, of the toleration of a government that adopted an Act of Parliament, July 1, 1664, demanding that all above sixteen years of age who should meet for purposes of worship contrary to the established form should be fined or imprisoned, and, for the third offence, should be banished seven years, or pay one hundred pounds, and, if they returned without leave, they should suffer death ? Is there any thing darker than this upon the statute-books of Massachusetts?

The clamors against the Puritans on the score of persecution are a modern excitement. They *are* to be blamed for it; but why blamed more than others? Is it because their virtues are so surpassing? Among the Chevaliers of Virginia, a law was enacted in terms almost identical with our most reprobated statute. Quakers should be subjected to close confinement until they should abjure their country; and, for a third return, they were to suffer death.

In evidence that the court at Whitehall did not at heart condemn our severities, we find a message from Charles II. to this colony, dated nearly a year after the celebrated *mandamus*. It contained these words: "Wee cannot be understood hereby to direct or wish that any indulgence should be granted to those persons commonly called Quakers, whose principles being inconsistent with any kind of government; wee have found it necessary to make a sharp law against them, and are well content you shall do the like there." These "sharp laws," as well as the simultaneous arrests in Holland, Russia, the islands of the Mediterranean, and the coasts of Algeria, all belonged to one great error, that belted the globe. Which misguided people is to cast stones at the rest? or is one alone to be selected for the assaults of all?

The peculiar character of the New-England

Plantation, **instead of aggravating** their crime, in **truth is a** real palliation **of it. They came into the** wilderness for the sole purpose of enjoying *their* religion without hurt or interference. The government was constructed with this object in view. " The Heart of New England Rent " refers to this fact as the very reason for its rigor. " The profession of the purity of doctrine, worship, and discipline is written upon the forehead of New England." **They** sought no proselytes ; and they did not endeavor to enforce their views beyond their **own** jurisdiction. " And now, " says Mather, " if the Quakers themselves had got into a corner of the world, and with **immense toyl** and charge made a wildernesse habitable on purpose to be undisturbed in the exercise of their worship, they would never bear to have New Englanders come among *them* and interrupt their publick worship and endeavour to seduce their children from it." The stern dealings of the State of Pennsylvania with some unpleasant intruders at the period in which he wrote seemed to justify this assumption. Beyond all question, a government has a right **to thrust** out those who interfere with **the very object** for which it was erected. The United States can suppress the Mormons. It was the evil practice of the age to proceed still

further, and attempt to control the opinions of
men.

But religion, their loved religion, was the object of the first communities in America. With
it the wounds of the outcasts were healed, and the
tears of their exile were sweetened. " New England was the colony of **Conscience.**" Every thing
was brought to the test of the higher law. Now here
were strange men who renounced, as they thought,
the authority of the Bible ; who denied the sanctity
of the Sabbath ; who called their holy ministry the
"seed of the serpent," and their dignified rulers
"monsters of iniquity ;" who alleged that an "inward light," which seemed from their conduct to be
a mere *ignis fatuus*, was the supreme guide of
every soul. It is difficult to say *what* should be
done with such a people. Certainly they ought not
to be slain. But is it a wonder, that, as the court
itself affirmed, " after all other means had failed to
check their impetuous and desperate turbulency,
the magistrates judged themselves called, for the
defence of all, to *keep the passage with the point of
the sword held towards them* " ? Their wilfully rushing upon it was their own act.

The Quakers, although they despised the sword,
were mighty with the pen. They have kept their suf-

ferings before the world. An almanac, prepared by
one of them for the year 1694, has this item of
chronology : " Since the English in New England
hanged their countrymen for religion, — years 36."
Their memory was relentless ; but we are glad to
acknowledge that their hearts were quick to forgive
us. There is beautiful evidence of this in a recent issue of the Massachusetts Historical Society.
It was found in the diary of Increase Mather
for the year 1676, a period of great distress to the
colonists, — this simple memorandum : " A vessel
from Ireland arrived here, *being sent by the Quakers*
in Dublin, for those that were impoverished by the
war here." Yet Quaker authors delight to de-
tail the woes they endured : their vivid narratives
fill many a capacious volume. They are perfectly
trustworthy as far as the facts they relate were
understood ; but they can hardly be said to give us
uncolored pictures. They are, however, our only
authorities for many of the cruelties alleged.
Thomas Westgate, writing from England to the
colony in 1671, said, " I dare not be an advocate
to plead for the cursed generation of Quakers ; yet
let me tell you New England suffers much in this
country for imprisoning many of them, — and
putting others of them to death, — and I could

heartily wish you had printed a narrative of your proceedure with them, together with the grounds thereof." It would no doubt have corrected some misconceptions.

The sufferers of that time used to predict that dire calamities would come upon their opposers; and they were fond of tracing out the deaths of their principal persecutors.

Major Humphrey Atherton, for example, had reviewed his battalion one afternoon on the Common, and in the dusk of the evening had started for home in "great pomp and pride." His horse on a sudden stumbled, and threw him upon the ground so violently that he was instantly killed, "near the place," observes Besse, "where they usually loosed the Quakers from the cart, after they had whipped them." "Being taken up, and brought into the Court House, the place where he had been active in sentencing the innocent to death, his blood ran through the floor, exhibiting to the spectators a shocking instance of the divine vengeance against a daring and hardened persecutor."

Richard Davenport, commander of the castle before Roger Clap had been appointed, in the heat of a sultry day, went into his room, and lay down upon his bed for a little rest. "There he was struck

dead in a strange manner, by thunder and lightning." Instead of regarding this event as a judgment of the Lord, should we not acknowledge the
special mercy which spared the whole company
quartered there, though only a thin partition separated the room in which he was killed from the
magazine of the castle?

Upon the accession of Charles II., John Norton
had been persuaded, much against his will, to sail
with Simon Bradstreet on a mission from the
Colony to the new king. They were graciously
received at the court, although the fears of the Colony had once reported that Norton was confined in
the Tower — for Charles had reason to be offended
with the men of Massachusetts. But George Fox
confronted them in London, as did also John
Copeland, whose ear had been cut off in Boston.
It was rumored likewise, "that William Robinson's
father was coming up from the North, to bring
them to account for murthering his son." The
Colonial agents were, however, not much troubled
by these annoyances, and returned safely to America
after their business was done.

Charles spoke honeyed words in his response.
" He received the Colonies into his gracious pro-
tection, and confirmed their patent and charter."

But there were other contents in his royal letter. He decreed that justice in the Colony should always be administered in his name, and that all persons of honest lives should be admitted to the Lord's Supper. These two articles would abrogate at a stroke the independence of their courts and the authority of their churches. They gave intense displeasure to the sensitive Colonists. "There were some who would not stick to say that Mr. Norton had laid the foundation for the ruin of all their liberties." He had done all that he could; but now he saw that some of "his best friends began to look awry upon him." He was not of a buoyant constitution. He drooped under these neglects. Hitherto he had always rode upon the topmost wave of popular favor. This change distressed him much in private, but did not alter the merit of his public course. He preached in his pulpit, and led the devotions of his church, with the same unparalleled eloquence as before. After returning from his accustomed services one Sabbath morning, he was suddenly seized with faintness, and fell to the floor entirely dead. The Quaker, with relentless hand, has written, "He was observed to fetch a great groan, and, leaning his head against the mantle-piece, was heard to say, 'The hand (or judgment) of the Lord is upon me ' " ! This heavy visitation was also considered a mark of divine vengeance ; but rather let us say with Mather, " Sudden death with him was sudden glory."

Rugged but **kind old** John Endicott must also **die.** For a long time he had been almost the only **one remaining, who could** describe, with the fond loquacity of a personal remembrance, what rude surroundings had **greeted that** forest-birth of the infant state. He was almost **the only** one who had seen it rise from its narrow **cradle to** the wider sphere of its vigorous youth. What miraculous transformations had unfolded before his eyes !

For the last sixteen years, he had been the counsellor and chief of the Colony. It had been a time of storm. But his fearless and unvarying hand had **held** a prompt and steady sceptre till the end. No man ever laid **it down** with more tranquillity and grace. He did not fall by an untimely blow. In the beautiful language of the day, " old age and the infirmities thereof, coming upon him, he fell asleep in the Lord, on the 15th of March, 1665," at the age of seventy-seven ; " and he was with great honor and solemnity interred in Boston," on the 23d of the same month. His frank and independent spirit, and the great services he had rendered the state, won their befitting guerdon in the public esteem. "He died poor," says the diary of Capt. John Hull, "as most of our rulers do, having more attended the public than their own private interests."

In the unflinching administration of what he thought to be justice, some men had suffered wrongfully; but, says Palfrey, "he understood *himself* to be severe, only in the assertion of an absolute right, and the needful exercise of a public guardianship." "For my country and my God," was the motto inscribed upon his motives. Unqualified devotion to the one, and unreserved obedience to the other, ever gave to his career a peculiarly buoyant and resolute advance. No faultless character is claimed for him. His steel-bound nature presented too few apertures for the appeals of the gentler emotions. Yet it may well be doubted whether men less stern in their principles than he could have accomplished, amid all the obstacles that they had to confront, the great work to which Providence had called them, — the foundation of a republic strong enough, ere long, to throw its radiant and solid arch across an entire continent.

"These transient persecutions," in the elegant phrase of Mr. Bancroft, "begun in self-defence,

were yet no more than a train of mists hovering of
an autumn morning over the channel of a fine river,
that diffused freshness and fertility wherever it
wound." If those mists have not altogether disappeared, we can look beneath them over wide and
blooming fields which that river continues to
enrich.

.

II.

THE WITCHCRAFT DELUSION.

II.

THE WITCHCRAFT DELUSION.

GALLOWS HILL still haunts the western border of Salem, a grim spectre of the dreadful past. Around its base have clustered the factories and homes of a thriving population, and their buildings begin to ascend its rocky sides. But the bald and ancient top continues to affront the open sky. Our eye cannot run up that rocky height, without recalling to our heart the most appalling event of Colonial history. There, looming against the summer clouds of 1692, nineteen innocent persons were hanged by the neck till they were dead. The witchraft delusion is not a myth. Its solemn witness stands to-day, reciting as it has from the first the weird story of its wild executions.

This is almost the only spot that can be identified with the tragedy that was then enacted. The subject was fraught with horror to the minds of the

original actors. Their faltering lips refused to repeat to their children the harrowing tale. Hardly
one oral tradition has come down from them to the
present day. How deep is the pathos of such a
silence! Those poor penitents avoided the theme
with studious dread, and in their daily converse
would pass and repass its local relics without a
word.

But over the broad earth there are many spots
that could speak to us in the language of Gallows
Hill, and those voiceless fields. Every nation,
every age, has brought its hecatomb of victims to
the altar of this imaginary crime. It was the lot
of our " City of Peace" to render one of the last,
though by no means the largest, of these offerings
of human life.

But why should a witch be hunted with the rude
vengeance which the records of the older times all
reveal? Can she be worthy of such severity? Our
modern notion of her is a very merry one. A
toothless, nervous old lady strides a broomstick,
and rides a wayward, rollicking race, over the trees,
among black clouds, stirring up little tempests of
wind, and landing we don't know where, and don't
care how. That is the witch of our ideas: why
strive to hurt her? To be bewitched now-a-days is

to be thrilled with a fascination that is pleasant instead of malign. It is not the effect of an "evil eye," but of glances that beam with innocent charms. With us a magical touch is a touch of delight ; enchantment bears the sense of Elysium. Perhaps we should not think it exaggeration to say that the Cupid of the classic story has surrendered his office to the first-class witch of our times. She brews no noxious poison but the philters of harmless love. She howls no horrid curses ; but she sings in siren tones. She has no "black art" to ply, aided by diabolic powers. With coy and unvexed management, she brings about her gladsome ends. How comes it to pass that such a dear, handy creature should have been condemned to die by the codes of every civilized country in the world?

Our reply to such a question must be briefly this. The meaning of the title was altogether different in former times from what it is now. It had ghostly terrors, of which the dawn of modern light has robbed it. We search for its definition. We are amazed to find that it embodies the most lurid notions that the mind has ever conceived. Dr. Ogilvie, in his learned revision of Webster to make the "Imperial Dictionary" of Great Britain, gives a

7

lustrous **description of its evil** import in the sev-
enteenth century. " Witchcraft is the practice of
witches, sorcery, enchantment, intercourse with the
Devil, a supernatural power which persons were
formerly supposed to obtain possession of by enter-
ing into *compact* **with the** Devil. Indeed, it was
fully believed that they gave themselves up to him,
body and soul, while he engaged **that** they should
want for nothing, and should be able to assume
whatever shape they pleased, to visit and torment
their enemies, and accomplish their infernal purposes. As **soon as the** bargain was concluded, the
Devil was **said to deliver** to the witch an imp, or
familiar spirit, to be ready at call, and to do what-
ever it was directed. By the aid of this imp and
the Devil together, the witch, who was almost al-
ways an old woman, was enabled to transport her-
self through **the** air on a broomstick or a spit, and
to transform **herself in**to various shapes, particularly those of cats **and** hares, to inflict diseases on
whomsoever she pleased, and to punish her enemies
in a variety of ways. The belief of witchcraft is
very ancient. It was universally believed in
Europe till the sixteenth century, and even main-
tained its ground with **to**lerable firmness till the
middle of the seventeenth century. Vast numbers

of reputed witches were condemned to be burned every year ; so that in England alone it is computed that no fewer than thirty thousand of them suffered at the stake ! " This great definition, pointed out to us by Mr. S. G. Drake, in his valuable introduction to a fine edition of Mather and Calef, is so clear and precise that we understand at once why *that* witchcraft was a capital offence. It was the very sin of sins. It was the most accursed iniquity, — nothing less than a personal league with the Evil One. It was not merely necromancy or magic, simply a wonder-working art. It was not the vague use of amulets and charms for the purpose of obtaining material good. It was not divination alone, which reads the thoughts of alien spirits, and turns the horoscope of coming events. It was not correspondence, by these means, with the unseen world, without regard to the character of the correspondent. This might be innocent. It might invite the intervention even of the pure angelic spirits. It might involve no great treason against God. But witchcraft was actual alliance with the prince of the power of the air. All nations then believed that mortal men, while still upon the earth, could become his pledged and formal confederates, and could join forces with him, and wicked spirits

beneath him, for the purpose of warring against
the gospel, and defying the King of heaven. Is it
strange that this was regarded as the most flagrant
of crimes? In acknowledgment of such a con-
tract, Satan, on his part, agreed to exercise his own
supernatural powers in their behalf, and also to give
to them the same powers, to a greater or less extent,
as they proved to be his worthy supporters.
Besides, this " covenant with hell " was thought to
convey great advantage to the Prince of hell himself as well as to his human accomplice. He could
not work with his best success in the sphere of this
world, without the voluntary co-operation of some
of its intelligent inhabitants. A bad man or a bad
woman, who consented to be an instrument for his
hand, was the mightiest weapon he could hurl
against the ranks of the good. To such a federation was ascribed almost unlimited power. " Thou
shalt not suffer a witch to live." If the seventeenth-
century notion is indeed the one the Scriptures
lodged in this word, no wonder the divine denuncia-
tion was proclaimed against it.

In the elaborate work of Mr. C. W. Upham upon
this subject, published by Wiggin & Lunt, the power
of a witch to afflict whomsoever she will is thus described : " She could throw them into convulsions,

cause them to pine away, choke, bruise, pierce, and
craze them, and even subject them to death itself."
She had the faculty of "second sight," and was
able to communicate information from the spirit-
world, like "mediums" of the present **day**. She
could read inmost thoughts, press temptations
upon those near or far away, bring up the shades
of the departed, and ply the living with **infernal**
arts of every kind. And, worst of all, she could
come in her "shape," or apparition, to any persons,
however distant from her "bodily presence," and
operate upon them as though she were really there!
It was this imagined fact which admitted the possi-
bility of "spectral evidence," as it was termed, —
evidence which proved to be the most disastrous
element in the Salem trials. Those persons who
were exercised by these malignant energies were
said to be "bewitched."

Now, had such a terrific system of beliefs a
groundwork in actual facts? No: we say boldly,
no. There is not one accredited instance of the
crime, as then understood, in all history, whether
sacred or profane. "The Witch of Endor" was
not a witch in their phraseology, but a conjurer
only, whom God assisted once by a miracle, to her
own great dismay. The Chaldeans and Magi had

7*

no kin to this tremendous being. The Roman augur and the Grecian pythia were ignorant as infants compared with such a seer. The fortune-teller was common-place, and the exorcist was confined to a narrow field of operations, when put beside our ancestral wizard. In such a presence, their power was weakness, and their guilt was piety itself. This crime was essential diabolism. Assuredly, it was never practised.

But, for two centuries, the whole Christian world *believed* that it was practised. This belief was a fountain of unutterable woe. We are driven to ask the question, How it was possible for those who bore the form of humanity to acquire such a fiend-like repute. How came they to be even charged with such iniquities?

Reginald Scot, an author who wrote so long ago as 1584, attempted to answer this inquiry in a rare and ingenious book, entitled " The Discoverie of Witchcraft." It was written, as the humane man observed, " in behalfe of the Poore, the Aged, and the Simple." Its kind and reasonable suggestions ought to have put the world' on guard against the errors into which it afterwards rushed. In a quaint and racy style, he describes the natural development of a hideous witch from misfortunes that

originally were not faults. "The **sort of such as**
are said to be Witches are Women, which be commonly old, lame, bleare-eied, pale, fowle, and full
of Wrinkels, poore, sullen, superstitious, and Pa-
pists, or such as know no Religion ; **in** whose
drousie minds, the Divell hath gotte a **fine** Seat.
They are leane and deformed, shewing Melancho-
lie in their faces, to the Horror of all that **see them.**
They are doting Scolds, mad, devilish, and **not**
much differing from them that are thought **to**
be possessed with Spirits." **Their mode of sup-**
port is precarious, he implies : "These miserable
Wretches are **so** odious unto all their Neighbors,
and so feared, as few dare to offend them, or **denie**
them any thing they aske. . . . They go from
House to House, and from Doore to Doore, for a
pot full of Milke, Yest, Drinke, Pottage, or some
such Reelefe, without the which, they could hardlie
live ; neither obtaining for their Service and Paines,
nor by their Art, **nor yet at the** Divel's Hands
(with whome they are said to make a perfect and
visible Bargaine), either Beautie, Monie, **Promotion,**
Welth, Worship, **Pleasure,** Honor, Knowledge,
Learning, or **any other Benefit** whatsoever."
Witchcraft does **not** pay, is **the view of** Reginald
Scot. But they become at length **hateful** to their

entertainers. "In the Tract of Time, the Witch weareth odious and tedious to her Neighbors; and they, againe, are despised and despited of hir, so as sometimes she curseth one, and sometimes another, and that, from the Maister of the House, his Wife, Children, Cattle, &c., to the little Pig that lieth in the Stie. Thus, in Processe of Time, they have all displeased hir; and she hath wished evil Luck unto them all." Soon after this is started the infernal suspicion. "Some of her Neighbors die or falle sicke, or some of their children are visited with diseases that affect them strangelie, . . . which, by ignorant Parents, are supposed to be the Vengeance of Witches, . . . according to the common Saing, "Inscitiae Pallium Maleficium et Incantatio," Witchcraft and Inchantment is the Cloke of Ignorance. . . . Also, some of their Cattell perish, either by Disease or Mischance. Then they upon whom such Adversities fall . . . doo not onlie conceive but are resolved that all their Mishaps are brought to passe by hir onlie Means." Now comes the trial. "The Witch on the other Side being called before a Justice, by due Examination of the Circumstances, is driven to see hir Imprecations and Desires, and hir Neighbors' Harmes and Losses to concurre, and, as it were, **to take** effect ; and **so confesseth** that she (as a Goddess) hath brought such Things to passe.   Wherein, not onlie she, but the Accuser, and also the Justice, are **sorelie** deceived and abused ; . . . as that she hath doone, or can doo, that which is proper onlie to God himselfe."

Are not these admirable touches of truth ?   But wise old Mr. Scot remained unheeded by the people.   For more than a hundred years thereafter, men conducted as though common sense upon this subject **had never entered a created** brain.   Literature upon it was abundant ; but, with hardly another exception, it only tended **to** exaggerate the false opinions already held.   Bright-hearted Horace, Mr. Upham shows, **was wise enough to** reject them.

> " These dreams **and terrors** magical,
>   These miracles **and witches,**
>   Night-walking sprites **or Thessal** bugs, —
>   Esteem them **not two rushes."**

But Virgil thus bemoaned his sickly flock, that **was** under **an** " evil hand : " —

> " They look so thin,
> Their bones **are barely covered with** their skin.
> What magic has bewitched the **woolly** dams ?
> And what ill-eyes behold the tender lambs ? "

Scot's work was burned by order of King James
of Scotland.   This redoubtable monarch then set
himself to writing his own book upon the subject.
It would have been well had he committed this
edition also to the same flaming sepulchre in which
he tried to bury the wiser words of his predecessor.
But the evil work was printed at Edinburgh in 1597.
Its title was simply "Dœmonologie."   Though
weak in thought, it was strong in credulity; and
its royal authorship made it a great power in the
kingdom.

Mr. Wright, in his "Narratives" (London, 1851),
has traced the origin of this momentous produc-
tion to the troubles that attended the wedding-trip
of the royal pair !

James was married to Anne by proxy while she
was still in her Danish home, and he in the lonely
palace of Holyrood.   As might be expected, the
royal spouse awaited the arrival of the new queen
with a good deal of impatience.   The return voyage
of the noble earl who stood as proxy, and was bearing the youthful bride to her anxious lord, was
vexatiously delayed.   The sea was tempestuous :
the ship acted as if she were "bewitched."   They
were driven, at length, in great stress, upon the
bleak coasts of Norway.   The bad weather con-

tinued : there was danger that they would be obliged to stay there during the entire winter. James could not endure the thought of so long a solitude. Summoning up more courage than it was his wont to exhibit, he set off in search of his wandering wife. He found her, at last, in Norway. They were again married *in persona*, and, at the re-appearance of spring, re-embarked for Scotland. After a very rough passage, they landed in the dominions of the king, May 1, 1590.

But such supernatural calamities as they had endured involved something mysterious. James was convinced that there was a conspiracy against him. Dr. Fian, a renowned magician, " register to the Devil," and his two hundred witches, had been plotting to drown their connubial Majesties ere they reached *terra firma !* Accordingly they were brought to trial.

The examination of these sad wretches then resounded through the kingdom. Agnes Sampsoun testified that she had acted in the following remarkable scene : Accompanied with a great many other witches, she put to sea one evening, each riding in " a riddle or cive, with flaggons of wine, making merrie and drinking by the way in the same riddles or cives " until they reached a kirk some distance up the coast. There they landed, "took hands on the lande and daunced this reill or short daunce, singing all with one voice, —

> 'Commer goe ye before, commer goe ye,
> Gif ye wall not goe before commer let me.'"

Then she confessed that one "Geillis Duncane *did* goe before them playing this reill or daunce, upon a small trumpe called a Jewes trumpe." James was so excited at this point, that he sent for Duncane, and obliged him to play over before the royal court the witches' reel upon a venerable jews-harp !

He expressed at one time some doubts about the truth of Agnes's marvellous stories. Thereupon "she declared unto him the very words which had passed between him and his Queen on the first night of their marriage, with their answers each to other ; whereat the King wondered greatly, and swore by the living God, that he believed all the Devils in Hell could not have discovered the same."

Though we are told the King "took great delight" in this trial, and "was made in a wonderful admiration," the end of it was tragical in the extreme. Dr. Fian was "byrnt" at the stake. Agnes Samp-

soun was taken to the castle-hill, and there bound
and "wirreit" (worried) until she was dead ; and
almost every one of the two hundred expired in
fearful tortures.

It was as a commentary on this great event that
the royal treatise was composed.   Such a work
could but have a wide and melancholy effect.   It
riveted the fetters of superstition upon the minds
of the people ; and, before a twelvemonth had
elapsed, it issued in the destruction of no less
than six hundred human lives, condemned for this
offence of witchcraft.

James came to the throne of England in 1603 ;
and he immediately propagated through his newly-
acquired realms the favorite hobby to which his
weak mind was devoted.   In the preface of a fresh
edition, he informs us of "the fearfull abounding at
this time in this country of these detestible slaves
of the devil, the witches or enchanters."   In consequence of this declaration, and of his unflagging
zeal, a new and terrible law was enacted, which
was not repealed for a hundred and fifty years. It
was the statute which formed the legal basis of the
proceedings at Salem.

Is it strange that measures like these, which
stamped a vulgar superstition with the authority of

8

law, and the advocacy of a king, should have rendered the belief in it well-nigh universal? But, prior to this, witchcraft had been pronounced a capital crime by the most venerated courts of the earth.

In 1484, the papal see (Innocent VIII.) issued a bull, charging the Holy Inquisition to pursue with pitiless vengeance all persons guilty of this iniquity. Successive popes re-affirmed his command ; and the pages of history are covered with the horrors which marked its bloody progress down the years for two centuries and a half. During the short space of three months in 1515, five hundred witches were burned at the stake in happy Geneva. For one hundred years, 1580 to 1680, in Germany alone, one thousand persons, on an average, *every year* were exterminated by the ravages of this imagined iniquity. Before its fatal march was checked, one hundred thousand souls had suffered judicial murder in that one country alone. Does this mammoth fact suffer the New-England tragedy of 1692 to stand out in solitary blackness?

Executions in Germany had hardly begun to abate, when they had entirely ceased in America. As late as 1749, a poor and witless nun closed the horrid drama there, by offering up her harmless life.

In the reign of Henry VIII., witchcraft was declared a felony of the deepest dye ; and Elizabeth signed a bill that imposed upon it the penalty of death.   It was not, however, until the accession of James that this monster chimera began its wild riot with thirty thousand victims, not one of whom it released until it had crushed him to death.   In 1647, nearly two hundred were executed in England for the crime of witchcraft.   Upon the testimony of Mr. Upham, we learn that several suffered death in Great Britain but a few years before the proceedings commenced at Salem.   Quite a number there were tried by the water ordeal, and were drowned at the very *time* the executions were occurring here ; and, some years *after* the New World had wholly recovered from its fatal mistake, a large number were sentenced and put to death in various parts of Europe.   It cannot be said that these foreign trials were conducted in any particular less perversely than our own.   Cruelty and superstition joined hand in hand ; and together they were ranging over the earth.

The frenzies which have generally laid hold of the popular mind have been unable to assail the best and loftiest spirits of the age.   Far over the surging error these clear-eyed watchers have sent forth a voice of wisdom, to guard men against the threatening storm.   But, in our studies of the witch-craft delusion, we discover no such pleasing relief. Rare spirits, the most gifted minds of the age in which they lived, have all been involved in this great ocean of error, which at one time enveloped the world.   In 1665, Sir Matthew Hale, who was universally admired for the purity of his character, and **his varied** and ample culture, presided at a trial in Suffolk County, England, which condemned two witches. The proceedings at this court, both on the part of the judge **and the** accusers, seemed to be patterns of **what** followed at Salem. The afflicted fell in **fearful** convulsions upon the floor. They **were dumb and** deaf and blind in turn, or all at once. They clenched their hands so furiously that the strongest men could not open them ; but, if by chance they barely touched the accused, on **a sud-**den they would fly apart, and the sufferers would utter piercing shrieks.

In order to see that this was not **a** counterfeit **distemper and cure,** several honored gentlemen took **a** child, while she was in her fit, to the farther part of the hall, and then conveyed Amy Duny, one of the accused, from the bar out towards the suffering maid. Having blinded her eyes with an apron, **a** third person touched her hand as though he was the accused. It produced the *same* effect as the touch of the witch did, before the court ! " whereupon the gentlemen returned, protesting that they did believe the whole transaction of this business was a mere imposture." Notwithstanding this, the prisoners were condemned. Sir Thomas Browne, a name of unrivalled celebrity in his time, appeared in the midst of this trial, and, having been invited to address the court, in an elaborate and ardent speech threw the whole weight of his powerful influence against the accused, and in favor of the reality of witch-craft. There seemed to be but one verdict from all concerned.

Reports of this famous trial were found in New England in 1692. There is no doubt but that it was regarded as the main text-book at the Salem court.

Men eminent in the church likewise held to this belief. Richard Baxter, our own beloved guide to the " Saint's Everlasting Rest," says, in his " Dying Thoughts," " I have many convincing proofs of witches, the contracts they have made with devils, and the power they have received from them." Don Villalpando, Advocate Royal in Spain, issued a work of four volumes on " Demonology and Natural Magic." It was republished by order of

8*

Philip III., under sanction of the Holy Inquisition. It established and defined the doctrines of witchcraft held by all the Catholic world. There was no particular of the proceedings here which does not find ample support in its details.

Towards the close of the century, several sagacious men probed deep the prevalent error, and, by their publications upon the subject, endeavored to drive it from the popular belief. But their arguments were not regarded until after the catastrophe was passed. Every man of this class was called "a witch advocate," or "a gallant of the old hags." Such reformers were, therefore, few and cautious. Witchcraft had the credence of Sir Edward Coke. It was countenanced by Lord Bacon himself. It was maintained in an imposing convocation of bishops. It was preached by the clergy everywhere. More, Calamy, Glanvil, and Perkins, honored ministers, wrote in support of its reality. The educated classes of America were no exceptions to this army of errorists. Nurtured in European institutions, of course they entertained European views. Jurists, physicians, magistrates, and clergymen, and the populace almost without dissent, believed in the theory and the practice of witchcraft, through and through. What was to protect a devoted village, when all the fury of this heaven-wide cloud should burst upon it?

Salem Village was the fair country seat of Salem Town. It was five miles distant, on the fruitful plains now occupied by Danvers Centre. It afforded rich farm-lands to the wealthier settlers, such as Governor Bellingham and Townsend Bishop. They still retained each his "house in town." But as the forests were cleared away, and the engrossments of agriculture increased, a neighborhood of yeomen was formed there which gradually became a permanent and independent community. In 1671, about forty years after the first grants of land were made, they organized a new church, separating from the First Church. Its ancient records, still preserved, are the chief source of the information we have concerning the witchcraft proceedings.

Among these sturdy freeholders, pending the settlement of boundary lines, many contests had arisen. Such had been the limitless expanse at the disposal of the court, that these lines in the original grants had been carelessly defined. But, with British vigor, each pioneer soon began to insist upon his personal rights. In some cases, trees were felled in the day-time by one claimant, which would be dragged off and stored for fuel in the night-time by his rival! Real violence occasionally ensued, as well as costly suits, which, of course, they could ill afford to meet. "The farmers" and the "Tops-field men" became at length embroiled in bitter feuds. These tended to sour their spirits, and were the seeds, it is thought, of the wild animosities of the witchcraft delusion. Parish troubles had also distracted the new society. The first minister, Rev. J. Bayley, through the eight years of his labor, encountered determined opposition. The second minister, Rev. George Burroughs, was opposed by the friends of the first (*antiquus mos!*), and, after a three years' struggle, had fled to a mission-field on the shores of Casco Bay. He was a modest, pure-hearted man, small of stature, but of amazing physical strength. Certain prodigious feats which he performed were afterwards the occasion of his doom. They were regarded as proof that he had a diabolical confederate. He was summoned back from Maine to be put to death, on the charge of witchcraft. Deodat Lawson was his successor. His pastorate was brief; but afterwards, at the very crisis of the spreading frenzy, he returned, and preached to his former people a sermon full of lurid picturings of the power of Satan, and stern denun-

ciations of those in league with him.   The whole
populace rushed from the church " exceedingly mad
against " the accused.

  In 1688 Rev. Samuel Parris became the pastor.
This is a name more loaded with odium than any
other of the age.   He was the *pontifex maximus*
of the witchcraft disasters.   It is not for us, however, to judge his heart.   By no means does it appear that Mr. Upham is right in referring his activity, through all this terrific drama, to avaricious
cunning, and a reckless determination to carry his
point in transactions with the parish.   Many things
look suspicious, it is true ; but there is not one that
is absolutely decisive.   He was a designing and
crafty man, no doubt ; a great manager, ambitious
for power, and vain of his parts.   He was, besides,
very credulous and fanatical.   He was a victim of
superstition.   But so was also the age in which he
lived.   Have we not seen that the *whole world* was
tinctured with the very infatuation which swept this
people on to utmost ruin ?   Our main position is,
that, in similar circumstances, arrest, conviction, and
death would have followed the charge of witchcraft
as swiftly and certainly in any other village of
Christendom as in Salem.   The reasoning would
have been the same everywhere.   It would have

been this : " Witchcraft, according to divine and human law, is a capital offence : the accused are guilty of it ; therefore let them be executed."

Prior to 1692, there had been executions for witchcraft in America. Margaret Jones was sentenced by the saintly John Winthrop, and hung in Boston in 1648. Ann Hibbins was sentenced by the revered John Endicott, and hung in 1655. The gentle William Penn presided at a trial in Philadelphia which convicted two Swedish women of the same offence. They escaped death by a loose phrase in their indictment, and not by any special favor on the part of their judge. Two residents of Springfield were condemned in 1652. They likewise evaded the penalty. Elizabeth Morse of Rowley would have been executed in 1680 but for the reprieve of the governor.

A case, however, occurred in Boston in 1688, which is supposed to have had direct bearing upon the Salem trials.

A fierce old woman, named Glover, in round language had cursed a little girl in Mr. Goodwin's family for accusing her daughter, who was a laundress, of stealing some linen. " She was one of the wild Irish," and no doubt, in her maternal exasperation, spoke with great vehemence. Soon after, the child fell into fits, which seemed " to have something diabolical in them." One of the sisters and two brothers followed her example, and, though apart from each other, would suffer in just the same place at the same time. " Their jaws, necks, shoulders, elbows, and all their joints," says Hutchinson, " would appear to be dislocated ; and they would make piteous outcries of burnings, cuts, and blows," the marks of which were afterwards visible. The wrathful woman was charged with " bewitching " them. She was accordingly executed.

The " Goodwin children " became so celebrated for their marvellous antics, that Cotton Mather took one of them into his own family, and endeavored faithfully to exorcise her. She must have been a wonderful adept in the histrionic art. For many days she played upon the good man's credulity with amusing adroitness. She gayly read off the abominable books of Quakers and Catholics, which the doctor earnestly hated ; but she could not decipher a syllable of the " Assembly's Catechism." She was struck dead at the sight of Cotton's " Milk for Babes," but doted on the " Oxford Jests." She was much in love with the Prayer-Book, but she shivered with horror at sight of the Holy Bible. She would whistle and sing and yell at family

prayers. She would riot in contortions and pains
of every description, now choked by an invisible
noose, now baked in an invisible oven, now chilled
in invisible water, while her face would blacken or
her skin would perspire with heat, or her shivering
body would be covered with goose-flesh. Mr.
Mather prepared a sermon upon the mysterious
developments. It created a profound impression.
It was published in a pamphlet, and distributed.
It easily filled the country with the belief that this
child was indeed "bewitched," — the victim of diabolical power.

Such accounts were considered ominous. They
were thought to be proofs that Satan, with his confederate fiends, was about to make an onslaught
upon the New World. Baffled in the other hemis-
phere, he would make his last stronghold in this.
Here was to be fought his most desperate battle
for final supremacy. The fearful struggle was at
hand.

Such was the state of feeling, and the posture of
affairs, when the outbreak occurred at Salem Village. Theories of law and medicine and theology,
the world over, recognized the reality of witchcraft.
The popular belief in it was intense enough to sus-
tain almost any imposition bearing its name. The

community likewise had local traits which were
peculiarly foreboding when considered in connection with such a superstition.   They had the vigor
of pioneers, and the unfaltering resolution of free-
men.   They had been accustomed to strife.   They
had been hardened by what they felt to be wrongs.
Above all, they had the *moral force* of the Puritans.
This had brought them across the ocean.   This
had armed them against the savage.   This had
carried them through many a conflict.   **They** believed that a new struggle was at hand, more
momentous **than any in which they** had **engaged.**
They believed in God.   He was the object of heartfelt homage.   His cause was theirs.   His cause
was imperilled, and to its rescue they rallied.

Said an author of that day, " The New Englanders are a people of God ; settled in those which were
once the Devil's territories, **he has** tryed all sorts
of methods to overturn this poor Plantation, and so
much **of the Church as was 'fled into this wilder-**
ness.'   But all those Attempts of Hell have hitherto
been Abortive :— wherefore the Devil **is** now making one Attempt more upon us, **an** Attempt more
difficult, more surprising, more snarled with unin-
telligible circumstances, than any that we have
hitherto encountered ; an Attempt so critical that if

we get well through, we shall soon enjoy Halcyon Days, with all the Vultures of Hell trodden under our Feet."

During the witchcraft delusion, they felt that they were confronting, face to face, the Prince of the power of the air. With this one idea, a stern, self-sacrificing people threw themselves into the pitiless contest. They determined to do battle to the end, —to give no quarter till their detested foe was driven from the land.

We do well, as students of history, to pause for a moment, and admire the uncompromising consistency of those brave men. We have charges of cruelty and fanaticism to bring against them. But there was heroism, yes, devotion, in the stand they took. We see them grievously deceived ; but we need not be blind to the virtues they still possessed. The distressing details cause us to exclaim against strange excesses, and condemn what seemed to be obstinate blindness. We must not apologize for their wanton disregard of counter evidence, and the dictates of common humanity. We cannot dis-abuse our minds of the belief that some of the wily actors wilfully *plotted* to keep up the excite-ment, and took advantage of this fatal frenzy for objects of personal spite ; but, with no desire to

extenuate the follies or deny the sins of our fore-
fathers, in reference to the mass of those who were
implicated in it we must still give it the name of
" *the witchcraft delusion.*"

An orator before the Historical Society finely
said, "The witchcraft madness was no doubt a
dreadful passage in a majestic movement of events.
Even here, however, the great difference between
the people of Massachusetts, and of other communities whose history bears no such stain, is, that what
both alike professed to believe, the former more
consistently and honestly acted out. Deplore as we
may the grievous infatuation, still, *more* even than
we lament and condemn that, may we not find
cause to applaud the brave and constant spirit
that never would quail before the awful delusion
that possessed it? Set upon by invisible and supernatural foes, they thought of nothing but prompt
defiance and inflexible resistance, and the victory
which God would give his people."

Mr. Parris had in his household at Salem Village several slaves. Two of them were "John
Indian" and his wife Tituba. These two were
natives of South America. They were saturated
with the wild superstitions of the race from which
they sprang. They infused pagan elements into

the existing fanaticism, even if they did not origi-
nate the entire convulsion. But a circle of young
girls, with whom these swarthy creatures had mysterious interviews, formed the habit of coming regu-
larly to the parsonage during the winter of 1691–
92. This circle used to meet for the purpose of
practising the arts of palmistry and magic. They
resembled as nearly as possible " the circle " of the
modern Spiritualists. They were, however, children ; and wise warning or sound correction would
have broken up their illicit proceedings. Cotton
Mather advised, at the beginning, that they be separated " far asunder, and he would singly provide
for six of them." Had this advice been followed, it
would have averted all the horrors of the Salem
Witchcraft. In addition to the Indian slaves, the
names of eleven girls are given who were members
of the circle. They are referred to continually, during the prosecutions, as the "afflicted children."
Elizabeth Parris was the daughter of the minister.
Although only nine years of age, she conducted a
leading part in the early stages of the affair. Before
it had progressed very far, however, she was judi-
ciously sent away from home. Abigail Williams, her
cousin, eleven years of age, lived in Mr. Parris's
family, and, from the beginning to the end, was one

of the most audacious accusers. Ann Putnam, twelve years of age, the daughter of the parish-clerk, must have been a child of astonishing precocity. Her prominence was so odious throughout, that the tomb in which she was laid, at an early death, has been religiously shunned ever since. The dying have often requested not to be laid by her side. Mary Wolcott was the daughter of the nearest neighbor, and the " way through " from her father's house to the parsonage plat can still be detected. She does not appear to have been the worst of the miscreant set, although her activity was noted and disastrous. Mercy Lewis, seventeen years of age, was a servant-girl. Her unfaltering purpose and skilful management throughout made her responsible for much of the distress which came upon the whole community. Others are less conspicuous than these ; but the whole circle seemed to move with entire unanimity in acts of reckless presumption and appalling malignity. " For myself," says Mr. Upham, " I am unable to determine how much in their conduct may be attributed to credulity, hallucination, and the delirium of excitement, or to deliberate malice and falsehood."

A few females, more elderly than these, occasionally attended the mischievous meetings, and finally

9*

became active in the accusations.   Before the winter had passed, the circle had grown to be experts in the illicit arts they practised ; and at times they would display their attainments, to the great amazement of spectators.   They crept slyly into holes, dropped unconscious upon the floor, made antic and unnatural gestures, and could writhe in dreadful contortions, and utter piercing outcries.   At first no mention was made of their tormentors.   Gradually, however, the attention of the families with which they met was fully awakened ; and ere long the whole neighborhood was filled with the story of their unaccountable behavior.   Their condition became worse and worse.   They excited the deepest sympathy.   Dr. Gregg, the village physician, was called. Baffled by the unknown symptoms, he gave it as his grave opinion that they were " under an evil hand ; " that is, that they were " bewitched."   This professional decision spread like wildfire.   The whole country around became alarmed.   Witchcraft was the all-engrossing tropic.   Multitudes thronged in to witness the tremendous convulsions of the " afflicted children."   A love of notoriety seemed suddenly to awake within them.   From that time, perhaps it was their controlling motive. Soon they extended their operations to more public

places.   Their loud outcries and awful fits disturbed prayer-meetings and the services of the
Sabbath.

On the 20th of March, Mr. Lawson preached in
his old pulpit.   He has left a description of his ex-
perience which only an eye-witness could have composed.   "There were sundry of the afflicted persons
at meeting.   They had several sore fits in the time
of publick worship, which did something interrupt
me in my first prayer, being so unusual.   After
psalms was sung, Abigail Williams said to me,
' Now stand up, and name your text!'   And, after
it was read, 'It is a long text.'   In the beginning of sermon, Mrs. Pope, a woman afflicted,
said to me, 'Now, there is enough of that!'   And
in the afternoon, Abigail Williams, upon my referring to my doctrine, said to me, 'I know no doctrine you had; if you did name one, I forgot it.'
In sermon time, when Goodwife C. [orey] was present, Abigail Williams called out, 'Look where
Goodwife C. sits on the beam, — her yellow bird
betwixt her fingers'!   Anne Putman, another girl
afflicted, said, 'There was a yellow bird sat on my
hat as it hung on the pin in the pulpit!'   But those
that were by restrained her from speaking loud
about it."

No wonder such performances "something interrupted" him, as they did all others in that sober Puritan audience. Instead of rebuking the disturbers, however, almost every one regarded them with pity and solemn awe. A few good people ventured to express their disapproval of the rude behavior. They would not go to church to listen to such outrageous insolence.

They were marked by the offenders for subsequent vengeance. Mr. Parris was greatly troubled. He summoned the neighboring ministers to his own house ; and there they spent a day in fasting and prayer, in view of these strange dispensations. The children performed before their eyes. The reverend gentlemen were amazed and confounded. They solemnly re-affirmed the opinion of Dr. Gregg. They declared it to be their full belief that the Evil One had confederates in that community, bewitching these poor girls. This second professional decision banished every doubt. " Society at once was dissolved into a wild and excited crowd. Men and women left their fields, their houses, their employments, to witness the awful unveiling of the demoniac power, and to behold the workings of Satan himself upon the victims of his wrath."

Prompted by the principle that the Devil could

operate upon human affairs only through the instrumentality of human beings in league with himself, the question in all minds, and on every tongue, at once became, "Who, who, are those among us in league with him, afflicting these girls?" For some time, the girls held back their charges. The excitement deepened, and the importunity increased. "Who is it that bewitches you?" was the demand now pressing in from every side. At length, timing the announcement with exquisite delicacy, and selecting the first victims with admirable skill, one after another cried out, "Good," "Osburn," "Tituba." Sarah Good was a poor, "bed-rid" beggar, broken down by ill-fortune, and the object already of many suspicions. Sarah Osburn, "a melancholy, distracted old woman," had lost her good estate by an unhappy second marriage. Her mind was shattered. For a long time, she had been unable to take care of herself. Gossip about her was rife in the community. Tituba was the Indian woman mentioned before.

On the 29th of February, 1692, warrants were duly issued against these three persons. The complainants were four respectable men in the village. It was no child's play with them: it was a war with the Prince of hell. When the examinations came off, a vast crowd assembled to witness them. It was necessary to adjourn from the village-tavern to the meeting-house. John Hathorne and Jonathan Corwin, two of the most reputable magistrates of the Commonwealth, conducted the examinations. With great gravity, and a solemn prayer, they entered upon their task. Sarah Good was first put upon the stand. The examination proceeded in the following form. The prisoner stands on a platform in front of the excited assembly. The afflicted children are all present, and alert. The magistrate puts his questions in this amazing style, —

"Sarah Good, what evil spirit have you familiarity with?"

"None."

"Have you made no contracts with the Devil?"

"No."

"Why do you hurt these children?"

"I do not hurt them."

At certain junctures, the girls fall down, "dreadfully tortured and tormented," not being able to look at the accused without a spasm. If, however, they are brought to her, and made to *touch* her, the diabolical fluid immediately darts back into the witch; and they are relieved at once. Such acting could but have an overwhelming effect upon the court and all assembled.   The proceedings would then go forward as though conviction was a foregone conclusion, and the evidence of the afflicted children absolute proof.

Tituba, the slave-woman, though denying at first the charge of witchcraft, afterwards acknowledged it.   They had searched her body, and found several hard scars.   They were said to be made by the Devil, but were, in reality, produced by the sting of the Spaniard's whip in South America.   She had obeyed, however, "the black man with a book." But she renounced her compact with him, and all its horrible obligations.   She described minutely her infernal operations ; and by her strange and awful fancies, suggested by her heathen youth, added much to the terrors of the occasion.   Her behavior was probably a part of the plot to drive on the delusion.   As soon as she confessed, the afflicted children were calm.   These three were all committed to jail for trial.

Among the evidences of witchcraft, one was the "witch-mark."   The Devil was supposed to affix this to the bodies of his confederates, as a seal, and afterwards that spot would become discolored or callous.   The law provides that it shall be

searched for.   At Salem, a committee for each
sect permanently discharged this odious and cruel
office.   They would test the supposed teat by
running a pin through it.   Some such dead or
darkened spot could be found on almost any
person.

Another class of testimony was called "spectre-
evidence."   It was supposed that the witches could
go to those whom they wished to afflict, in the like-
ness of any animal, — a dog, a hog, a cat, a rat,
a toad ; or any birds, particularly yellow-birds.
They could likewise go in their own apparition,
however far away their actual body was.   This
power was also recognized in the books of law.
With such evidence admitted, the defence of an
alibi was entirely void ; and no charge could be
disproved which the imagination could invent.

A witch could also act upon her victims at a distance by means of "puppets."   These were little
bundles of cloth in any form, or amorphous.   Whatever was done to the puppet would be suffered by
the party bewitched ; for example, a pin stuck in
it would pierce the flesh of the person.   A bottle
of old rusty pins is preserved in the Court House at
Salem, said to have been taken from puppets and
the bodies of the afflicted children.

But to resume : the excitement was not quelled by these commitments. Tituba had mentioned four others as engaged with her in their Satanic occupations. Two were already in chains. Who were the other two? The girls continued to be tortured. Ere long, " they cried out upon " another : this was Martha Corey, a pious, sweet-tempered lady, wife of old Giles Corey. Her only fault was her disapproval of the actions of the girls. She also was committed ; the accusers, at her examination, executing some of their rarest feats. The success they achieved in this case emboldened them. Their next victim was a lady without a superior in social esteem and religious character, — Rebecca Nourse, a venerated mother in Israel. Several times during the examination, the magistrates seemed about to give way to the moral effect of her conscious innocence : it was only by the most tumultuous convulsions that the accusers could keep them firm. She was at length committed.

All caution seemed now to be abandoned. A mere infant, four years old, was next imprisoned for the crime. The Devil had effected a lodgement in Salem Village : this was the overwhelming thought in every mind. At this juncture, Deodat

Lawson arrived in town, and preached his ever-memorable sermon.

He took for his text Zechariah iii. 2. **He** pictured the grim warfare of Satan : he called upon God's people to rally against him. The effect of his discourse was immense : awe, anger, consternation, and frantic zeal, all were augmented in the hearts of the hearers.

It was truly a masterly **effort : its** imagery was sublime and terrific. **The sum**mons to confront unflinchingly their hellish foe was **in** the highest style of impassioned eloquence. At once it was printed, and distributed throughout the land. **Mr.** Parris also took occasion to preach upon the all-engrossing theme.

It was sacramental day. He announced for **his** text this awful charge, " **Have** I not chosen you twelve, and one of you **is a devil?** " The sister of Rebecca Nourse was present, — a noble-hearted sister, who could not endure such a fling against one who had sat with her, she knew, in sincere and sacred communion at the table of the Lord. She was then chained in a noisome dungeon, awaiting the horrors of a frenzied tribunal. Sarah Cloyse's heart was full : she could not stay in such a lying company. She rose at once, and passed out of the meeting-house to her home.   The congregation were greatly amazed ; but so runs the relation of one who was there.   " She was afterwards seen by some in their fits, who said, ' O Goodwife Cloyse, I did not think to see you here!'   And, being at their red bread and drink [that is, at a diabolical feast], said to her, ' Is this a time to receive the sacrament?   You ran away on the Lord's day, and scorned to receive it in the meeting-house ; and is this a time to receive it?   I wonder at you.'"   Well might they " wonder " at the bare idea of a pure and pious lady like Sarah Cloyse mingling in the festival of devils?   Why did it not seem so strange to her neighbors as to be wholly incredible?

But charges were renewed against prominent persons.   A special " council " came down from the General Court to examine them.   This was an imposing procedure.   The council consisted of the deputy governor and five other magistrates. They came displaying all the insignia of office, and forms of State.   It was a great day for Salem. The entire population were out.   They crowded into " the great and spacious meeting-house," where the grand judiciary was held, instead of at the village. At such a crisis as this, nothing could have been more imprudent than such an extraordinary act.

It added **fuel to the** flaming excitement **of the** masses **who** gazed upon it. For a preliminary examination, **simply** with a view to commitment, it **was** unnecessary and reprehensible in the highest degree. Sarah Cloyse was the accused, together **with** Elizabeth Proctor. The inquisition of the **"council"** was teasing and frightful. The powers of **the prisoners** failed. Sarah Cloyse sank down "in **a dying fainting fit,"** and weakly **called** for water. "Her **spirit,"** screamed the band of the afflicted, "is gone **to** prison to her sister Nourse"! Goodwife **Proctor** was charged with having urged one of the **girls to sign the** Devil's book. "Dear child!" exclaimed **the** accused in her agony, "it is not so." **"There is another judgment, dear** child!" Then the **accused turned upon** her husband, and declared that **he, too, was a wizard. All three were** committed, **April 2, 1692.**

The witnesses, in their evidence, had ascribed most blasphemous actions to the prisoners. They painted the infernal sacrament in lurid colors. **The** Devil was ministrant, these poor creatures **were deaconesses, and** *their own blood* was the wine. **It is passing strange** that their youthful imagina**tions** were capable of inventing such awful false**hoods.** As the testimony came out, all present were

horrified : it tended **to** deepen their **resolve to pun-**
ish the fiendish crime.   Four more were committed
April 19.   One of these four was old Giles Corey.

This man had a peculiar repute in our gossiping
community.   He was a singular character.   Some-
how he had got a bad name.   But it does not ap-
pear that he deserved it.   He simply dared to disregard the conventional manners of the day.   He
ventured to be odd.   He cared not a whit for the
small talk and the small customs of those about
him.   Until 1659, his home was in Salem Town.
For thirty years, however, he had been a farmer **of**
the Village.   The farm contained **more** than **a**
hundred acres of excellent land, and he owned
meadows also near Ipswich River.   The con-
tract with his carpenter for building his house is
still preserved.   It was to be " twenty feet **in**
length, fifteen **in** breadth, and eight feet stud."
Mr. Upham, in his vivid manner, refers in this connection, to the general size of houses in those days.
One of Winthrop's letters describes a tempest,
"than which I never observed a greater," which
blew off the roof of Lady Moody's house and all
the chimney above it.   So sound were the slumbers
of that peaceful time, that " Ten persons lay under
it, and knew not of it till they arose in the morn-

ing!" But the fact comes out, that this fine lady's house was flat roofed, of one story, and nine feet in height!

Corey had had many a rough passage in his life. He was a bold man, of exuberant physical strength. He was not inclined to surrender his point, even though he was obliged to resort to violence in order to maintain it. Yet he had a generous and forgiving nature. He was careless about avoiding "the appearance of evil." Going into town one day with a cart-load of wood, a neighbor met him, and shouted out, "How now, Giles : wilt thou never leave thy old trade? Thou hast got some of my wood here upon thy cart." Corey answered "True, I did take two or three sticks, to lay behind the cart to ease the oxen because they bore too hard." Such peccadilloes, repeated frequently, furnished constant material for the scandal-mongers.

A hired man, named Goodell, fell sick at his house in the winter of 1676. He was at length carried home to his friends by Goodwife Corey. Soon after he died. It was whispered about, that he had come to his death in consequence of an awful flogging, given him in a passion by Corey. Corey was brought to trial for murder. There was evidence to show that the poor man had been beaten in his own family after his **return**; though it could not **be** denied, that, for a certain fault, he had been severely chastised by his former master. Yet as no cause for ill-will was manifest, and Corey's wife had given him the best of care, notwithstanding the prejudice **against** the accused, he was finally discharged. This affair came up again, however, in a far different court from that.

John Gloyd, another laborer on his farm, was a man of sullen and unforgiving temper. They had fallen out with each other a number of times; but, in 1678, a quarrel between them **about** wages had grown so fierce that they resorted to the law. The case was, however, taken out of court, and put into the hands of referees, mutually chosen. It was decided against Corey by the voice of John Procter, who was the friend of Gloyd. The loser expressed himself perfectly satisfied, and, in his elastic, generous way, enjoyed a **treat** over the affair with Procter; "for they drank wine together, and Procter paid for part, and Corey for part."

But a few days had passed, when, one morning before daylight, Procter's house took fire, **and was** burned to the ground. There seemed to be men about the neighborhood always eager to lay every evil thing that happened to poor Corey's account.

He was **accused of being the** incendiary, and was indicted for trial. By incontestible evidence, an *alibi* was proved, and Corey was triumphantly acquitted. He thought however, from this high-handed attempt to wrong and ruin him, and from statements at the trial hinting at other current calumnies, that it was time for him to put a stop to the malignant and mischievous slanders which had been flying about concerning him. He instituted proceedings against quite a number of witnesses for defamation of character, and recovered damages against them all. This sharp course, however, did not put his maligners into permanent good humor.

But, **for fourteen years after this event,** the hard-working but healthy old man lived in comparative peace. He was now an octogenarian. He had **been** married three times. Four daughters, children of his first wife, were all the mistresses of happy households around him. His present wife, Martha, was a woman of prayer. Through her loving influence, no doubt, the weather-beaten, " weary " husband was led to the throne of heaven-ly grace. The consolations of religion began to cheer his long-troubled heart. When the silver of more than eighty years was mantling his head, he advanced to the altar, and made a profession of his

faith in the Saviour.   In his confession to the First
Church, the one with which he united, he spoke
of his "scandalous life."   His humble words were
entirely satisfactory to the Christians there, and he
was received to cordial fellowship.   His trials
seemed at length to have reached a termination.
With a peaceful hope in a happy home he was pre-
paring to die.   But, just before he entered the
haven of eternal repose, a storm, more lurid with
lightnings and more furious with deadly gales
than he had ever encountered, lashed the sea
around him, and drove him in its awful rage right
upon the rocks.   He was wrecked in the fearful
surge.

When his wife was first arraigned for witchcraft,
he was himself a firm believer in the prevalent delusion.   She, however, had been one of the two or
three persons in the entire community who had the
sense and boldness to declare "that she did not
think that there were any witches."   A committee
from the church called upon her with suspicions
raised by the outcries of the afflicted children.   She
received them in a smiling manner, and said, "I
know what you are come for : you are come to talk
with me about being a witch ; but I am none"!
They did not "get on" much in their interview,

and left her thoroughly convinced of her knowledge of the Scriptures and of her sprightly politeness.

But her "shape" continued to torment the girls. She was brought before the magistrates, and, despite all her virtues, was promptly committed. While undergoing her final trial, with serene and firm composure, she re-asserted her disbelief in the delusion. All the wiles of the crafty girls could not confound her; and she listened to her sentence with a heart undismayed by the terrors it denounced.

"Sister Martha Corey," runs a record in Mr. Parris's Church book, after her condemnation, "was this day in public, by a general consent, voted to be excommunicated out of the Church." The pastor and three brethren carried the vote to Salem prison. "Whereupon, after a little discourse, and after prayer, which she was willing to decline, the dreadful sentence of excommunication was pronounced against her." At length she was carried to the scaffold. Calef tells us that "Martha Corey, protesting her innocence, concluded her life with an eminent prayer upon the ladder."

We cannot refrain from inserting here part of a very quaint but plaintive ballad, which appeared in a Salem paper many a long day since. How

true it is that pleasantry and pathos may be **linked**
in one subtle thought!   Irony may also hide a keen
point in the feathery stuff.   **The author is** name-
less.   The piece has **been rescued** from oblivion by
the vigilant Mr. Drake, and is in the safe custody
of his opulent work on Witchcraft.   We have room
for a few lines only.

> Come all New England **men,**
> And hearken unto me,
> And I will tell what did befalle
> Upon yᵉ Gallows tree.

> In Salem Village was the place,
> **As I did heare them saye,**
> And Goodwyfe Corey was her name,
> Upon that paynfull daye.

> **This Goody Corey was a** witch,
> **The** people did believe,
> Afflicting of the Godly **ones,**
> Did make them sadlie grieve.

> There were two pyous matron dames,
> And goodly maidens three,
> **That cryed** upon this heynous witch
> As you shall quicklie see.

> And when before the magistrates
> For tryall she did stand,

This wicked witch did lye to them
While holding up her hand.

" **I** pray you all good gentlemen,
Come listen unto me,
I never harmed those two Goodwyfes
Nor yet these Children three.

" **I** call upon my Saviour Lord
(Blasphemously she sayed),
As witness of my innocence,
In this my hour of **need.**"

The Godly ministers were shockt,
This witch prayer for to hear.
And some did see yᵉ Black Man there
A whispering in her eare.

She rent her cloaths, she tore her haire,
And lowdly she did crye,
" May Christ forgive mine enemies
When I am called to dye ! "

Dame Corey lived but six days more,
But six days more lived she,
For she was hung at Gallows Hill
Upon yᵉ Locust tree.

No doubt **the husband of** Martha Corey was at
first much shocked at her repudiation of all belief
in the doctrine of witchcraft. It was thought by

the most eminent minds that such unbelief was little better than blank infidelity.

A member of the Royal Society in England, but a few years before, had written, " Atheism is begun in Sadducism. And those that dare not bluntly say, ' There is no God,' content themselves, for a fair step and introduction, to deny there are spirits or witches ! " Richard Baxter said, about the report concerning the " Goodwin children " " The evidence is so convincing, that he must be a very obdurate Sadducee who will not believe."

Around the family altar, therefore, Giles Corey had probably spoken sharply to his wife, and rebuked her for this lack of faith, in his rough, impetuous way. Perhaps he had likewise made imprudent speeches abroad, and, in his vexation, had fallen into his life-long phrases, saying that " she acted as though the Devil was in her."

A strange paper has been preserved, which was evidently prepared for use against her at her trial. It was abandoned, however ; for although it shows that Giles believed himself, and every thing about him, to be " bewitched," he was not willing to say that his own wife was the witch. It runs thus :—

" The evidence of Giles Corey testifieth and saith, that last Saturday evening, sitting by the fire, my wife asked me

11

to go to bed. I told her I would go to prayer, and when I
went to prayer I could not utter my desires with any sense,
nor open my mouth to speak. My wife did perceive it, and
came toward me, and said she was coming to me. After
this, in a little space, I did according to my measure attend
the duty. Some time last week, I fetched an ox, well, out
of the woods, about noon, and he laying down in the yard I
went to raise him, to yoke him ; but he could not rise, but
dragged his hinder parts as if he had been hip-shot. But
after, did rise. Another time, going to my duties, I was interrupted for a space, but afterwards I was helped according
to my poor measure. My wife hath been wont to set up
after I went to bed ; and I have perceived her to kneel down
on the hearth, as if she was at prayer, but heard nothing ! "

Such a document could serve no purpose at
court ; but what an inlook it gives to the fireside
of those two artless old people ! There was the
calm and experienced Christian matron, making the
" hearth " her closet of prayer, at an hour when no
one would intrude ; and there was the bluff, un-
chastened convert, who had come late to a religious
life, whose mouth had long been used to sentiments
not akin to devotion at all. No wonder the poor
old man was not an adept in " uttering his desires " !

Why the girls selected him for their outcries cannot be told? Perhaps, since his wife's actual commitment, a re-action had taken place, and he had

manifested his abhorrence of their duplicity.   Certain it is, that, if he felt this abhorrence, he would have expressed it without fear or favor.   His examination was in the meeting-house of the Village.

"Giles Corey," said Hathorne, the magistrate, "you are brought before authority upon high suspicion of sundry acts of witchcraft.   Now tell us the truth in this matter."

"I hope through the goodness of God I shall; for that matter I never had no hand in, in my life."

"Which of you have seen this man hurt you?"

Four of the girls at once affirmed that he had hurt them.   And they proved it on the spot by spasms and awful convulsions.

"What was the reason," said Goodwife Bibber, "that you were frightened in the cow-house?" And then the questionist was suddenly seized with a violent fit.   "I do not know any thing that frightened me!"   All the afflicted were seized, now, with fits, and troubled with pinches.   Then the court ordered his hands to be tied.   "What! is it not enough to act witchcraft at other times, but must you do it now, in face of authority?"

Overwhelmed by the dread displays before him, involving so much mystery, and evoking the sympathy, even of his aged heart, he answers, "I am a poor creature, and cannot help it." **Upon the** motion of his head again, they **had** their heads and necks affected. Thomas Gold testified that he heard him say that he knew enough against his wife that would do *her* business. "What was that you knew against your wife?" The holy courage of his spirit began to rise. The **reply** befitted the most **heroic martyr of** that sad time. "*Why, that of living to God, and dying to sin!*" "One of his hands was let go, and several were afflicted. He held his head on one side, and then the heads of several of the afflicted were held on one side. He drew in **his** cheeks, **and the cheeks of the** afflicted were **suckt in."**

One testified something about "temptations he **had had to make way with himself."** This revealed **the** fact that a dark struggle had been going on in his mind. Perhaps he was almost driven to suicide by the recollection of the little part **he** had performed **in** bringing his wife into her awful condition, and his greater part in driving on the public frenzy. Little did he think then of that mode of "making **way** with himself," to which his splendid will at length should rise, and which was ever after to be lauded in the annals of this delusion as its most guiltless and glorious act.

At the same time he was committed, Mary Warren was sent to jail. She had been one of the most violent accusers. She was suddenly one of the accused. What was meant by this new move? She would be a spy in the enemies' camp, to warn and aid the girls from that point. Her part was planned for her, no doubt, by the malignant "circle." She acted it out with deliberate cunning from the first. Her apparent defection would indicate, it was thought, that the girls were not acting in concert. She suffered herself to be convicted, that she might avert suspicion from the rest, while they continued to play their high and dangerous game. Four prisoners, who were comrades with her during her confinement, made a deposition to this effect : —

" We heard Mary Warren several times say, that the magistrates might as well examine Keysar's daughter, that had been distracted many years, and take notice of what she said, as well as any of the afflicted persons."

As if to avert suspicion of her own imposture, she spoke afterwards of her distempered head, which from time to time would be filled with shapes that tortured her. But, when her public trial came on, she was wholly on her guard. She solemnly affirmed that she had formed a league

11*

with **Satan.** **She had** "signed his book." At the timely moment, however, then and there, she renounced her **league** forevermore. Her confession was wild with fragments of imagined conversation with the Evil One, and was often broken by fits of **long duration.** Mr. Parris, reporter of the case, makes this memorandum : —

"Note, that not one of **the sufferers was** afflicted during her examination, after once she begun to **confess,** though they **were** tormented before."

Her struggle with Satan was long and fearful, **before she could tear herself from his** desperate **clutches.** At length she was victorious ; and then **she gave such a** circumstantial and horrid exposé **of the sins of witchcraft,** that it confirmed the faith **of the eager listeners in** its reality, and cleared her easily of all its punishments. She acted her part with dexterous address.

In descriptions of the diabolical sacrament, **a** "**man** in black" had been spoken of. Who was this? **High and** dreadful disclosures were expected in the response. **They** were truly at hand, **when Rev.** George Burroughs was declared a witch, **— this term** being then applied indiscriminately to males and females. He was laboring in his humble field in Maine ; but they despatched the sheriff, arrested him rudely, and committed him for trial. Nothing could have prompted this selection but pure and simple malice. There was existing, however, an old parish-grudge, which leagued well with a desire on the part of the accusers to show the fearful power they could wield.

The prisons now were almost full of those who had "signed the book" of the Devil, putting themselves in solemn federation with him.

In the town of Andover, a good man's wife fell sick. He became convinced, by the physician attending, that she was "bewitched." He drove down to Salem Village to ascertain from the "afflicted children" who was her tormentor. Two of them returned with him to Andover. "Never," says Mr. Upham, "did a place receive such fatal visitors. The Grecian horse did not bring greater consternation to Ancient Ilium. Immediately after their arrival, they succeeded in getting more than fifty of the inhabitants into prison, several of whom were hanged !" Panic spread everywhere. The idea prevailed, that the only way to prevent an accusation was to become an accuser. The confessing witches were thus greatly multiplied, and the power of the delusion mightily strengthened. Fear was on every face, and distress in every heart.

Many quit the country altogether. Business was at a stand-still. The conviction settled upon the people that an infernal confederacy had got foothold in the land, and was carrying it over to the power of the Evil One.

At this crisis, May 14, 1692, Sir William Phips arrived in Boston with a most momentous commission. The government, under the old charter, was abrogated ; and the new charter, making Massachusetts a royal province, instead of an independent colony, commenced its unwelcome sway.

Rev. Increase Mather, who had been the agent of the State at the royal court for five years, was invited to nominate the officers of the incoming administration. Phips was appointed governor at his suggestion. Concerning his character as a ruler, Hutchinson slyly says, " His conduct when captain of a ship-of-war is represented as very much to his advantage ; but further talents were necessary for the good government of a province." Had he been a great-hearted man, he might, in the exercise of his newly-acquired power, have done much to assuage the growing frenzy. Instead of that, he sent a petty, cruel order down to the jails of Salem, requiring that those imprisoned for witchcraft should be thrown into irons at once.

A scrap from the account-book of John Arnold, the jailer, has recently been found. It has these significant items : " **May 23.** To shackles for ten prisoners ; " " **May 29. To one pair** of irons for **Mary Cox** ; " &c. At this time, the prisons in all the vicinity of **Salem were** full. There had been no final trials at all. Urged by a sense of the emergency, although he had no shadow of authority for the act, the governor constituted a special Court of Oyer and Terminer. **It was made up of** seven judges, **armed with** his commissions. **The** deputy-governor, William Stoughton, was chief-justice : most of its members were citizens of Boston. They were impartial men, if any could **be** found ; although, like their fellow-citizens, they were bond-slaves of the delusion.

The court was opened at Salem in the first week of June. And now the scenes **of the** preliminary examinations were to be repeated **at a more** august tribunal. The character of the evidence was the same ; and the futility of all defence, with the existing laws, was quite as apparent.

Bridget Bishop was the only one tried at the first session. She was a weak, irascible woman, although in respectable life, — occupying the very house in town where the honored author, Mr. Upham, afterwards resided.   She was convicted by the fits and fancies of the girls ; and, within a week, the dreadful sentence was executed on Gallows, or Witch, Hill.

After this first brief act of the bloody drama on which they had entered, the court withdrew to take breath.   They wished to examine their position. It was found that there was no statute in the Province in actual force against witchcraft at the time of the commitments.   The old enactment of James the First was regarded as sufficient authority.   Just as the special court were upon the point of adjourning, the General Court revived the laws of the first charter, dated 1641.   The one against witches was very concise : "If any man or woman be a witch (that is, hath or consulteth with a familiar spirit), they shall be put to death."   These laws were drawn up by the celebrated John Cotton.   They are termed "The Body of Liberties."   In the margin, against this paragraph, are the references, Deut. xiii. 6–10, xvii. 2–6 ; Ex. xxii. 20.   By this action, the Legislature adopted the proceedings at Salem as a Provincial matter, for which the immediate locality was not responsible, but the country at large.

During the recess of the court, the Governor

and Council **presented a** request to the prominent clergymen of **the** metropolis for their advice **in the** existing state of **things.** Mr. Hutchinson gives **us the famous document** entire. **It conveys** the **calm** opinions **of the** cultivated and pious **men of** the day.

*The Return of several **Ministers** consulted **by his** Excellency and the Honorable Council upon the present Witchcraft in Salem Village.*

BOSTON, June 15, **1692.**

I. The afflicted state of our **poor** neighbors that are **now** suffering by molestations from the invisible world, **we ap-**prehend so deplorable, that we think their condition calls for the utmost help of all persons in their several capacities.

This justified their intervention.

II. We cannot but, with all thankfulness, acknowledge the success **which the merciful God has given to the** sedulous and assiduous endeavours **of our** honorable rulers to defeat the abominable witchcrafts which have been committed in the country, humbly praying **that** the **discovery** of those mysterious and mischievous **wickednesses may be** perfected.

This was a courtly compliment.

III. We judge, that, in the prosecution of these and **all** such witchcrafts, there is need of a very critical and *exquisite caution,* lest, by **too** much credulity for things received only upon the *Devil's authority,* **there be a** door opened for a long train of miserable consequences, and Satan get an advantage over us ; for we should not be ignorant of his devices.

This is royal advice. Would that it had been followed !

IV. As, in complaints upon witchcraft, there may be matters of inquiry which do not amount unto matters of presumption, and there may be matters of presumption which yet may not be matters of conviction, so it is necessary that all proceedings thereabout be managed with *exceeding tenderness* toward those that may be complained of, especially if they have been persons formerly of an unblemished reputation.

Shall we find this "tenderness" in the Salem court ?

V. When the first inquiry is made into the circumstances of such as may lye under the just suspicion of witchcrafts, we could wish that there may be admitted as little as possible of such *noise*, company, and openness, as may too hastily expose them that are examined, and that there may be nothing used as a test for the trial of the suspected, the lawfulness whereof may be doubted by the people of God, but that the directions given by such judicious writers as Perkins and Bernard may be observed.

Perkins gives sixteen rules for discovering witches epitomized in "Wonders of the Invisible World," London, 1862, p. 30. Any man to-day would willingly be tried by them, if fairly applied.

VI. Presumptions, whereupon persons may be committed, and much more convictions, whereupon persons may be condemned as guilty of witchcraft, ought certainly to be more considerable **than barely the accused persons being** represented by a *spectre* unto the afflicted ; inasmuch as it is an undoubted and **a notorious thing, that a dæmon** may **by** God's permission **appear even to ill purposes in the** shape of an *innocent,* yea, **and a virtuous man.   Nor can** we esteem alterations **made in the** sufferers by **a** look **or touch of** the accused to **be** an infallible evidence of guilt, but frequently liable to be abused by the Devil's legerdemain.

The ministers fought against "spectre evidence ;" **but it** *was* **in fact** the only fatal **evidence** that was rendered at all.

VII. We know not whether some remarkable affronts given the devils, by **our** disbelieving those testimonies, whose **whole** force and strength is from them alone, may not *put a period* unto the progress **of** the dreadful calamity begun **upon us, in** the accusation **of so many persons,** whereof some, we hope, are yet clear **from the great transactions laid to their** charge.

" A period " **would have been** put to it, had they obeyed this clerical suggestion.

VIII. Nevertheless, **we cannot but** humbly **recommend** unto the government **the speedy and vigorous** prosecutions of such as have rendered themselves obnoxious, according to the directions given in the laws of God, and the wholesome statutes of the English nation, for the detection of witchcraft.

This was **the** only recommendation obeyed by the magistrates in any particular.

Such was the renowned "advice " of the foremost preachers of New England to its representative lawyers. Are the principles here announced more bitter than the practices of that bar to which they were sent ? Did they aggravate the existing frenzy ? Did they not rather by every paragraph, except the last and those written for the sake of courtesy, — by every paragraph *protest* against the legalized excess of the day ? It wrongs the ministry of New England to lay upon them a heavy burden of blame for the agonies that were then endured. They believed in witchcraft, it is true ; but they always lifted their voices for moderation and kindness.

Cotton Mather himself, who has been called the " prime instigator " of those gloomy prosecutions, was the author of this advice from the ministers. In a long letter written by him, May 31, 1692, to John Richards, one of the judges, before the first sentence of death had been pronounced, he "most humbly begs him in the management of the affair, not to lay more stresse upon pure spectre testimony than it will bear," saying, " It is very certain, that the divells have sometimes represented the shapes of persons not onely innocent, but also very vertuous." He was even afraid of being accused as an apologist of the sin. " Perhaps there are wise

and good men, that may be ready to stile him, that
shall advance this caution, *A Witch Advocate;* but, in
the winding up, this caution will certainly be wished
for." Devoutely it was wished in " the winding up "
that it had been heeded !

And he even advanced the almost heretical
notion, that a plain confession may not prove the
confessor a witch. "A person of a sagacity many
times thirty furlongs lesse than yours, will easily
preceive what confession may be credible, and
what may be the result of only a delirious brain or
a discontented heart." No custom was more common than to test the accused, by requiring him to
repeat the Lord's Prayer. If he made the slightest
slip, it was counted as evidence against him. In
the preliminary trials, one had stood the embarass-
ing test perfectly, except that she had said unwit-
tingly, " Deliver us from *all* evil." Here was supposed to be a petition designedly perverted to in-
clude the punishment to which she was justly
exposed. In another attempt, she blundered more
impiously, saying, " Our Father which art in heaven,
hollowed be thy name ; " a petition that God's
name might be *void* and dishonored, and "so a
curse rather than a prayer." But Cotton Mather
said of this experiment, " Make no evidence of it,

but onely use it for confounding the lisping witches to *give a reason* why they cannot, even with prompting, repeat those heavenly composures." He goes one step farther, and suggests a venturesome notion for his day, saying this: "It is worth considering whether there be a necessity alwayes by exterpaccons by halter or fagott (to punish) every wretched creature that shall be hooked into some degrees of witchcraft; what if some of the lesser criminalls be onely scourged with lesser punishments?"

This invaluable letter, which has come to light in a recent publication of the Massachusetts Historical Society, shows conclusively that the reverend author was not a hard-hearted fanatic, but an earnest, thoughtful seeker for a bloodless deliverance from the impending fury.

Thirty years after, we find him still in advance of his age, advocating, at the risk of his life, the practice of inoculation as a safeguard against small-pox. So odious was this reform to the medical world, that one man, at least, became his mortal foe. He threw into his room a hand-grenade, which would certainly have killed him, had it chanced to explode.

But his indefatigable pen, which, before he died, had written 382 books, wrote on unchecked. This resolute sentiment was then inscribed : " A spiteful town and poisoned country can't extinguish my poor studies to do good in the world!"   Says Mr. Poole, "The ministers generally, and he especially, favored inoculation, basing their arguments on medical science.   The doctors, with one exception, opposed it with the utmost vehemence, on theological grounds. **The** ministers and the lawyers had stood in about this relation respecting **the** legality of witch trials."

The delicate sense of Mr. Longfellow, **whose melodious** verse suggested this little book, discerned, among the first of modern scholars, the real truth about Mather's relation to witchcraft.   The words he put into the mouth of this remarkable man are **not sharp and bloody** words, but those which **are** eloquent with great compassion and grief.

The frequent journeys which he made at that time from Boston to Salem were designed for the tender ministrations of the prison-cell, and not to goad on the attorneys of judgment.   Their pace was too swift for him already ; and we have the most affecting evidence that he was often welcomed to the dungeons **of the doomed.**

But we do not claim for the author of "Wonders of the Invisible World" exemption from the com-

12*

mon delusion. If he was more kind, he was also
more credulous, than most of his time. He believed that devils were actually abroad in many a
tangible human frame. This business, he wrote,
though " managed in imagination, yet may not be
called imaginary. The effects are dreadfully reall.
Our deare neighbours are most really tormented,
really murdered, and really acquainted with hidden
things, which are afterwards proved plainly to have
been realityes."

But is it wise for us of to-day to laugh at the
notion that there was any thing mysterious in
those appalling scenes? A merry old English judge
might dispose of a crazy and scared wretch, who
was pronounced a witch because of the romantic
fact that she had ridden a broomstick through
the air, with such a happy sentence as this:
" That she was free to go, and to ride broomsticks as often as she pleased; for he knew no
law against it "! But here was something more
than broomsticks and aerial journeys. Preternatural events were exhibited daily before the eyes of
multitudes of sensible and honest people. No
doubt there was much fraud and mischief mingled
in with these manœuvres, especially of the girls;
but, sifting this completely out by rigid research, will

there not still remain a **residuum of** unexplained mystery?

A contemporary author, whom **Mr. Chandler** quotes approvingly, cannot be **charged** with great extravagance in the **following assumption:** " Flashy people may burlesque these things ; **but when** hundreds of the most sober **people, in a country** where they have as much mother-wit certainly **as the** rest of mankind, know them to be true, nothing **but the absurd and** froward spirit **of Sadducism can question them.**"

It is a doctrine of calm philosophy, that the spiritual and **natural worlds,** acting **and** re-acting upon each other, **are separated by** the thinnest veil. While enthusiasm **alone credits all the marvels** which fly **to our ears, that is a stolid mind** which denies the existence **of every** thing it **is not able** to fathom.   Would not men be **better to believe in all** the sprites that have peopled the **realm of fancy,** rather than to believe **that there is nothing in the** universe but dust?. **When our** senses are shut, there is a world **to be** observed, which is beyond the senses when they **are** keen-sighted and awake. With the glad vision of eyeless Milton, we rejoice to find companions in every solitude.   **It is a beau-**tiful thought, —

" Millions of spiritual creatures walk the earth
Unseen, both when we wake and when we sleep."

In the last week of June the court met again :
five were tried and convicted at this session.
They were all hanged July 19. One of these
was Rebecca Nourse. Her distinguished virtues
and saint-like bearing staggered the jurors, as they
had the magistrates before. In spite of the monstrous testimony of the accusers, the clamors of the
outside crowd, and the bias of the court itself, they
brought in a verdict of " Not guilty." The wrest-
ing of judgment at this point seems amazing to us.
Immediately all the children and others afflicted,
within and without the court, set up a hideous out-
cry, and wallowed in horrible antics. One judge expressed himself dissatisfied, then another. Then the
chief-justice, who, though a man of rectitude, always
seemed to be bent on convictions, suggested that
one petty item of testimony had not been duly considered, and sent the jury out again : they returned
with a verdict of " Guilty." Surely justice had fled
from that court.

There is a tradition, that the body of this poor
woman was sought out, under the secrecy of night,
and borne in tender arms across the fields to the
burial-plot next her own home. Her sunken grave

still is pointed out, and the oaken house in which she lived still stands.

On the 5th of August, six were tried and condemned. These were all executed on the 19th, excepting one. Rev. George Burroughs, John Proctor, and George Jacobs, Sen., were among this ill-fated band.

Mr. Burroughs was condemned for "certain detestable arts, called witchcraft and sorceries, by which Anne Putnam was and is tortured, afflicted, pined, consumed, wasted, and tormented." At times the children appeared to be struck dumb by his malign power. "What hinders these witnesses," demanded Stoughton, "from giving their testimony?" "I suppose the devil," Burroughs replied. "How comes the devil," was the grim retort, "so loath to have any testimony borne against *you?*" He had murdered his two wives, who had already died, and also the wife and daughter of Lawson, his successor as village-pastor. The man was thunderstruck at such unheard-of lies. Said Ann, "One wife he stabbed under her left arm, and put a piece of sealing-wax on the wound; and she pulled aside the winding-sheet, and showed me the place"! He was chaplain at the diabolical banquets of the time. And with these

spectral fancies were also mingled strange stories
about his monstrous strength, "being a little man."
He had " lifted a gun of six-foot barrel, putting the
fore-finger of his right hand into the muzzle of said
gun," and holding it out at arms' length, "only with
that finger."   He had also taken up "a full
barrel of molasses with but two of the fingers of one
of his hands in the bung," and carried it "from the
stage-head to the door at the end of the stage."   It
is doubtful whether he was condemned for murder
or for lifting a " barrel of molasses."

In company with others he rode in a cart to the
fatal hill.   Upon the ladder he made a calm and
powerful address, refuting the folly of the day
" with such solemn and serious expressions as were
the admiration of all present."   He then offered
up a wonderful prayer, concluding with the Lord's
prayer, which he repeated correctly with thrilling
intonations.   Such was his "fervency of spirit,"
that many were affected to tears, and were at one
time resolved to prevent the execution.   But, at
this moment, "the accusers said the black man
stood by and dictated to him ;" and so the rising
sympathy was quelled, and the man of God went to
his long home.

It was well known that a confession of witchcraft,

and a formal renunciation of it, would **clear the**
accused from its fatal consequences : those only
who denied their guilt were obdurate wretches ;
others relenting were released. " More than one
twenty confessed that they had signed unto a book
which the devil showed them, and engaged in his
hellish design of bewitching and ruining our land."
Now, we need not assume that these confessions
were the result solely of the instinct of self-preser-
vation. They were not all deliberate falsehoods.
In that dread storm of delusion, when masses of
horror hung like inky clouds over every **home, and**
a thousand preternatural sounds reverberated in
every ear ; when **a** wife and a daughter beloved
could accuse the husband and father of the accursed
sin, and nearest **and** dearest friends — as was actually the case **in several** instances — were the
most positive in their charges, especially when
summoned to confront at the court a multitude of
faces, pale with fury or with fright, and to account
for the more appalling and ghastly antics of the
girls, — it is more than probable that some were self-
deceived, and really believed that they were agents
of the diabolical powers. But still more honor is
due to those who stood firm in such a trial. They
proved themselves possessors of minds that were

wise and strongly poised, and of characters that were **truly** sublime. The men who steadily refused to **take** that lie upon their lips earned well the **name of** martyrs, — noble martyrs to the very spirit of truth. Witch Hill is the Smithfield of America.

A petition, signed by a great majority of the neighbors of Proctor, was presented at court in his behalf : it is evidence to show that the severities **of the** prosecutions are chargeable, not more upon the community of Salem than upon the government at large. He never would have been condemned had their will had its way. Mr. Proctor wrote a letter from his prison-cell to five of the most prom- **inent clergymen in the** State, imploring their in- tervention for a new trial, and a change of magis- trates. These clergymen were *known* to be opposed to the excesses of the prosecutions. In- crease Mather **was supposed, in** heart, to disapprove **them** altogether. Samuel Williard, of the Old South Church in Boston, "one of the most revered and beloved ministers in the land," was so notable in his opposition to them, that the "afflicted children" actually began to "cry out upon" him. They were speedily hushed by the incredulous court. "Indeed," says Mr. Upham, "the truth is, that the judges, magistrates, and legislature were as much to **blame** in this whole business **as the** ministers, and much more slow to come to their senses and make amends for their wrong-doing."

During September, fifteen were tried and convicted : eight of these were executed Sept. 22. Rev. Mr. **Noyes,** of the First Church in Salem, turning to the strangled bodies, is represented to have said, " What a sad thing it is to see eight firebrands of hell hanging there ! " It was the last time that his eyes were pained by such a sight.

Three days before, old Giles Corey had suffered a fate that shocked the hearts **of** all good men. He had refused to plead to his indictment, and so was pressed to death.

His object in this refusal was to *prevent* a trial. He knew it could issue in nothing but a conviction. It would certainly fasten upon his name the stigma of a felony : **it** would forfeit the right of his children to his estates.

During the time of his imprisonment, waves of **painful** remembrance had rolled upon his soul. His life, he thought, had issued in little good ; he had been always misunderstood ; his influence had been all wrong, though his heart was often right. Since his conversion, there had not been time enough to approve the sincerity of his new profes-

sion. **And then that** martyred wife ! Though he
had never been opposed to her personally, yet the
delusion to which he had at first lent himself so
violently had swept her away. Two of his sons-
in-law turned against her in that hour of her extremity. With unnatural hearts, they even urged
her conviction. Sadly musing on all these facts,
his mind gradually settled upon a lofty resolve.
He determined to expiate his errors by a deed that
would challenge **the respect** of his fellow-men, and
that would perhaps, with **an** irresistible voice,
rebuke the iniquitous court : at least, it would save
his property to his children. Forthwith he caused
a deed to be drawn up in the prison. It was done
with the utmost formality, to make certain the effect.
It conveyed to Cleaves and Moulton, the two sons
who had been **true to his** wife, his entire estate of
" movables **and** lands." It was **signed** and sealed
in the presence of competent witnesses, and duly
recorded as a complete transaction. Then he was
ready to attest his determination not to break this
instrument by the attainder **of a** felon's death.
He made up his mind not to be tried.

He was summoned before the court to plead to
his indictment, " Guilty," or " Not Guilty." He uttered not one word in reply. There he stood mute

as a stone: and no power upon the earth could unseal his iron lips. To have pleaded would have recognized the legality of that tribunal, and have made him, in some sense, a party to their proceedings. They represented the passions of the deluded multitude. He defied their right to give judgment. That dumb mouth spoke in thunder-tones of remonstrance.

When Giles Corey took this immovable position, but one course seemed open to the court. The usage in England was to give the recusant three separate opportunities to plead, each time announcing the dread penalty of continued contumacy. After the third trial, if he still remained speechless, he was remanded to prison, with the sentence of *peine forte et dure.* He would then be thrown upon his back, and weights of stone or iron would be piled upon him. There he would be kept, sometimes for days, the weights gradually increasing, until the sufferer had consented to plead, or had been pressed to death.

No details of this enormity — once only committed in our land — have come from the recess of that prison-cell in Salem. The rumor is, that the closing scene of the tragedy was in a secluded field near by; that the heroic man told them it was no use

to expect him to plead, they might as well pile on
the rocks at once.   And so they did; and so he
died, — an old man of more than eighty-one
years, — braving the utmost torture that the human
frame can bear, until his body was crushed, and
his unconquered spirit had fled forever away.

A part of the weird ditty quoted before refers
to this heroic death: —

> "Giles Corey was a wizzard strong,
>   A stubborn wretch was he ;
>   And fitt was he to hang on high
>   Upon yᵉ Locust Tree.
>
>   So when before yᵉ Magistrates
>   For tryall he did come,
>   He would no true confession make,
>   But was compleately dumbe.
>
>   'Giles Corey,' said yᵉ magistrate,
>   'What hast thou heare to pleade
>   To these who now accuse thy soule
>   Of Crymes and horrid deed?'
>
>   Giles Corey, he sayde not a word :
>   No single word spake he.
>   'Giles Corey,' sayth yᵉ magistrate,
>   'We'll press it out of thee.'
>
>   They got them then a heavy beam ;
>   They layde it on his breast ;

They loaded it with heavy stones;
And hard upon him prest.   ·

‘ More weight,’ now sayd this wretched man :
‘ More weight,’ again he cryed.
And he did no confession make ;
But wickedlie he dyed.”

This horrible event was one of the last acts in
the tragedy.   It was too much for a compassion-
ate people longer to enact.   At this point, we
would that the curtain of oblivion might fall, and
hide the whole black past from our view.   But the
hand of remorseless history drags it aside.   We
must recognize that past as a veritable transaction
in the annals of our Puritan State.

Mr. Upham makes much of the artful adroitness
with which the order of incidents was arranged,
and the supplies of excitement were furnished at
the critical moments throughout.   He thinks that
some power behind the scenes, perhaps in Ann
Putnam's family, perhaps Mr. Parris himself, managed the dreadful drama from the beginning.   There
would be reasons for such a suspicion, did it not
involve a personal depravity so inhuman as to be
almost incredible.   There was, indeed, a sequence
of events calculated every way to intensify the
frenzy.

13*

But at length the tide was to turn : Reason was to resume her sway. The girls, over-estimating their power, struck too high. They could not make the people believe that Rev. Mr. Williard was guilty. Then a member of Increase Mather's family was accused. Then the wife of Sir William Phips himself, was "cried out upon." Finally, the wife of Rev. Mr. Hale of Beverly was charged with the crime. This act seemed to break the spell. She was a lady known in all the region round, — one of such eminent graces, that it *could not* be that she was a witch. Mr. Hale had been a leading, and, we believe on his own confession, a sincere prosecutor ; but he *knew* that his wife was innocent, and, he turned at once his powerful influence against the current. *The accusers had perjured themselves :* this conviction spread suddenly through the community. The people had been duped. It was all a mistake. Oh what a mistake ! And the wild storm quelled. In a moment that mortal delirium was checked. The whole delusion vanished.

Gov. Phips saw that a stop must be put to the prosecutions. The Court of Oyer and Terminer met no more. The Superior Court, which met in January, 1693, convicted only three out of fifty indicted. These three escaped execution.

Other trials resulted uniformly in acquittal.   In
May, the Govenor, by proclamation, discharged all
who were imprisoned for witchcraft.   " Such a jail-
delivery was never known in New England."   The
number set at liberty was about **one** hundred and
fifty.   Two had **died** in prison.   **Twenty,** including
Giles Corey, had been executed.   Many had escaped from confinement.   In all, there must have
been nearly three hundred arrested and committed
for this imaginary crime.

The calamitous effects of the delusion were **long**
and painfully felt.   Those **pure and** precious **lives**
could not be recalled to **earth.**   From many a
household, domestic happiness had forever fled.
The retrospect indeed was fearful.   Gentle women
had been torn from **their** families to suffer the
rigors of a public trial, if not judicial death.   Laboring men had been arrested in their needful toils.
The industry of the youthful State had been crip-
pled.   A whole summer had been lost to the hus-
bandmen.   Their fields had been left unploughed,
and they had no harvests to gather in.   The
excitement of the hour consumed every other
interest.   It left them destitute at its departure.

Confidence in the safeguards of the community
had also been disturbed.   **The** pro**tecting** hand of

the General Court had not defended the innocent. The **calm voice of** science had become an accuser. The **white** ermine of justice had been stained by needless blood. The altars of our holy religion had afforded no asylum to the distressed. Law-givers, physicians, magistrates, and ministers, instead of repelling the woful superstition, had **united together to strengthen it.** It was not well for the various causes they maintained. There was hardly one social **good which** was not injured by the shock it then received.

But, amid all that is sorrowful in this dark scene, **there are** facts which stand out in the pure and pleasant light.

One is the genuine penitence of those misguided men. It is beautiful to us. Most of the girls turned out ill. Several of them became profligates. Only one, Ann Putnam, made a confession. Chief-Justice Stoughton clung proudly to the position that his decisions were right throughout. Some few of the clergymen contended to the end of life that these were veritable " wonders of the invisible world." **Mr.** Parris was never known to repent the part he performed. He was soon forced to leave his charge on account of the prejudice then engendered. He died in obscurity. But, with these exceptions, the rest of the prosecutors made most honorable acknowledgments of the injuries they had done. Their expression of feeling was not immediate. Great sorrow sealed their lips. Words, they feared, would kindle the rage, rather than soothe the grief, of those who had suffered such remediless wrongs. But their action at length was unequivocal.

In 1696, a proclamation for a public fast was issued, especially in view of "the late tragedy," that "God would humble us therefor, and pardon all the errors of his servants and people. That he would show us what we know not, and help us wherein we have done amiss to do so no more." It is couched throughout in most affecting terms.

Nearly fifty years after, the General Court adopted a measure, appointing a committee to inquire into the condition of those families which might have suffered in "the calamity of 1692;" reversing the attainders, and expressing a strong desire to compensate them either by money or a township of land.

The two churches which had been most deeply implicated tearfully revoked the sentences which had excommunicated those convicted of witchcraft, "that they be no longer a reproach to their mem-

ory, and an occasion of grief to their children."
They conducted with marked kindness towards the
surviving friends. The clergymen of Essex County,
with but one or two exceptions, signed a petition,
begging that the infamy of a criminal trial might
not rest on the accused, or appear on the court-
records.

And the twelve jurors, whose verdict had been
the doom of so many guiltless persons, united in a
declaration, subscribed by them all, expressing their
grief for what they had done. This remarkable
paper exhibits the utmost tenderness of conscience,
and asks forgiveness of God and men in terms of
such heartfelt contrition that it disarms our indig-
nation altogether.

But the conduct of Judge Sewall claims our
special admiration in this respect. Through his
whole life, after that fatal court, he observed annu-
ally, in private, a day of humiliation and prayer, in
view of his participation in it. On the day of the
general Fast, he rose in his own pew in the Old
South, in Boston, and, before the whole congregation, proceeded to the pulpit, and handed the pastor
a written confession of the wrong into which he had
been led, and an earnest request that his brethren
would unite with him in devout supplications that

it might not **bring** down the displeasure **of God** upon his country, his family, or himself. He re- mained standing during the **public reading** of the paper.   Such an example of noble penitence throws a bright gleam over all that melancholy past.

And now, may not the descendants **of** a **godly** ancestry, while they **recall the melancholy** errors by which the Fathers were **beset, be allowed, in the** same spirit of trust which distinguished them, to cherish the belief, that even this tragical calamity was permitted for purposes of wisdom and **benevo- lence ?** When such a moral desolation sweeps over a great society of men, it does not leave them **with- out** some beneficent results.   The thunder-storm does **its work ; the atmosphere is** cleared ; the sun shines forth at length, revealing not only **the spoils** of death, but the pure elements of a better life.

And what was God's good design in permitting this outbreak of a fatal superstition ? **For** our answer to such an inquiry, we are pointed at **once** to a great fact, which soon became apparent : *by that very fury the superstition itself was* **forever** *ex- ploded.* No gentler means than this, perhaps, could have accomplished such a **happy end.**   It may be, that those appalling enormities were necessary to drive out the deeply-lodged error from human beliefs. We of the present day need not treat it with ridicule or reproaches. In the seventeenth century it was invested with an awful solemnity. It is not for us to denounce that generation. All delusion has not yet departed from the earth. There are false and fatal systems of belief among many men to-day. We pray that they may not require so terrible a refutation as did this. But arguments seem powerless to destroy them. In the well-chosen words of another, " Error is seldom overthrown by mere reasoning. It yields only to the logic of events." The learning and wit of all the world combined could not have rooted the witchcraft superstition out of the minds of men. A practical demonstration of its deformities and horrors, such as was held up then to the view of the people everywhere, alone could give it a death-blow. This was the final cause of the witchcraft delusion. It makes it one of the greatest landmarks in the moral history of mankind It makes it a fair and trustful augury that God is leading humanity, by *every* providence, out of the gloom of ages, into the cloudless lustre of the " golden year."

www.ingramcontent.com/pod-product-compliance
Lightning Source LLC
Chambersburg PA
CBHW021122020726
47500CB00003B/877